A new stallion for ...dale...

Ashleigh stared suspiciously at the man's retreating form. Even though she desperately wanted Renegade for Edgardale, she could understand why Mr. Rolland would up his price after the great race the colt had run. But why would he suddenly change his mind and accept their offer?

Elaine Griffen looked around the car in disbelief. "Well, then, I guess we did just buy ourselves a horse after all."

"Yes!" Ashleigh cried. She pumped her fist in the air, deciding to cast aside her suspicions about the shady trainer. It really didn't matter what made him change his mind, she decided. The important thing was that he had, and Renegade was coming to live at Edgardale!

Collect all the books in the Ashleigh series

ASHLEIGH'S Thoroughbred Collection

THOROUGHBRED

Ashleigh

DERBY DREAMS

CREATED BY

JOANNA CAMPBELL

WRITTEN BY

CHRIS PLATT

HarperEntertainment

An Imprint of HarperCollins Publishers

HarperEntertainment
An Imprint of HarperCollins*Publishers*
10 East 53rd Street, New York, NY 10022–5299

This is a work of fiction. The characters, incidents, and dialogues are products of the author's imagination and are not to be construed as real. Any resemblance to actual events or persons, living or dead, is entirely coincidental.

Produced by 17th Street Productions, Inc., an Alloy Online, Inc., company

ISBN 0-06-106672-9

HarperCollins®, ▲®, and HarperEntertainment™ are trademarks of HarperCollins Publishers Inc.

Cover art © 2001 by 17th Street Productions, Inc., an Alloy Online, Inc., company

First printing: March 2001

Printed in the United States of America

Visit HarperEntertainment on the World Wide Web at
www.harpercollins.com

❖ 10 9 8 7 6 5 4 3 2 1

To Gen and Vern Balsi,
thanks for the wonderful friendship

1

"Anyone want to see the races at Turfway Park this weekend?" Derek Griffen called out as he rounded the corner of the barn. Eleven-year-old Ashleigh Griffen looked up from the wheelbarrow she was busy loading with dirty bedding.

"Sure!" Ashleigh and her little brother, Rory, chimed at once. Even their older sister, Caroline, who wasn't really interested in horses, enjoyed going to the racetrack.

"What's the occasion?" Ashleigh asked, tipping the wheelbarrow and dumping the soiled straw onto the pile. She handed the cleaning tools over to Rory and gave her father her undivided attention. They didn't get to go to the racetrack very often. "Does Mike Smith have a horse running?" Ashleigh hadn't seen the kindly trainer for a while, but she always liked to talk horses with him.

Mrs. Griffen reached out to help Rory steady the

wheelbarrow. "I believe Mike does have some horses running, but this is something special. Your father has a surprise for everyone."

"What is it?" Rory asked excitedly, blowing a lock of reddish blond hair out of his eyes.

Mr. Griffen shrugged. "You'll just have to wait until tomorrow," he said mysteriously.

"Oh, Dad." Ashleigh groaned. She pulled off her wool hat and shook out her dark brown hair. It was the beginning of March, and the weather was definitely getting warmer.

"It'll be worth waiting for," Mrs. Griffen promised.

Ashleigh began stuffing hay nets with sweet-smelling grass hay as she tried to figure out what the surprise would be. She hoped it had something to do with the Kentucky Derby.

The Derby was the most famous horse race in the country. Each year over a hundred thousand people crowded onto the grounds of Churchill Downs on the first Saturday in May to watch the big race. Edgardale, the Griffens' Kentucky farm, was only a breeding farm, but Ashleigh had always hoped that one day Edgardale would keep one of its best Thoroughbred foals to raise and race in the Kentucky Derby. So far, she hadn't been able to talk her parents into it.

Ashleigh glanced at her father, trying to read his

face, but he just winked at her and cut open a bale of hay with the wire cutters. She knew she'd get no more hints from him.

Ashleigh helped her family finish the rest of the chores, then made a quick stop by her own horse's stall before going up to the house for dinner. "You're going to turn into a big carrot if I don't stop giving you so many of these," Ashleigh told Stardust, watching the chestnut mare munch her treat.

"Guess what?" Ashleigh said, running her hand down Stardust's long white blaze and looking into her inquisitive eyes. "I think Mom and Dad are getting us tickets to the Kentucky Derby."

Ashleigh continued down the aisle to give a treat to Moe, a little Shetland-Welsh-cross pony. The molasses-colored pony had once been Ashleigh's, but she had outgrown him, so he was Rory's now.

Ashleigh laughed as Moe stretched his fuzzy head over the door to accept the treat. The pony resembled a small bear with his thick winter coat. She was glad Rory would have the job of brushing him when he started to shed.

Ashleigh turned at the sound of approaching footsteps. Jonas, Edgardale's only hired hand, rounded the corner and flipped on the barn lights against the gloom of the coming evening.

"The rest of your family went up to the house to dinner," Jonas said. "If you don't hurry, there won't be anything left, and you'll be stuck down here, eating with the horses."

Ashleigh laughed. "Caroline made dinner tonight. If she's tried one of her experiments again, carrots and sweet feed might taste better."

Jonas smiled. "I'll fix you hot bran mash right now," he teased.

Ashleigh hurried toward the house, but she stopped halfway down the aisle and turned back to Jonas. "You know what the surprise is, don't you?"

Jonas plopped his hat back on his head and grinned. "And if I told you what it was, it wouldn't be a surprise anymore, would it?" He nodded toward the house. "Your family's waiting."

Ashleigh left the barn, stopping to look out across the acres of white-fenced paddocks that surrounded Edgardale. She smiled dreamily. Soon the new shoots of Kentucky bluegrass would be poking through the ground and the paddocks would be filled with broodmares and their new foals. Maybe one of this year's foals would be the Derby horse she had always dreamed of.

She stuffed her hands into her jacket pockets as she strode toward their old, white two-story farmhouse.

Tomorrow's races seemed like an eternity away. She hoped she could find something to do to make the time pass more quickly.

Ashleigh pulled open the front door and stepped into the hallway. She wrinkled her nose at the smell of burned cheese and frowned. It looked like she'd be spending most of her night cleaning up Caroline's burned cooking pans.

Saturday morning seemed to drag out forever, but finally the Griffens piled into their old station wagon and headed down the highway to Turfway Park racecourse. Since the track was a two-hour drive away, Ashleigh had brought a stack of *Daily Racing Forms* to study. Rory colored in his coloring book, and Caroline flipped through the pages of a teen magazine.

Ashleigh wished her sister would take more interest in the horses, but Caroline preferred painting her nails to a good gallop over the fields on a fast horse. Ashleigh was thankful her best friend, Mona Gardner, who lived on the farm next door to Edgardale, was just as into horses as she was. Ashleigh had promised to call Mona as soon as they returned to Edgardale. Mona was as anxious as she was to learn about Ashleigh's parents' surprise.

Ashleigh listened to her parents converse, hoping that she could glean some small clue about their secret. But they were being careful not to reveal anything. When they finally turned off Interstate 75 and onto Turfway Road, the air in the car was tense with anticipation.

Rory put down his coloring book and clapped. "We're here! So where's the surprise?"

"Not so fast, partner." Mr. Griffen laughed as they pulled into the parking lot on the back side of the racetrack. "Let me get the car parked first."

Ashleigh's heart quickened. They usually went immediately to the front side of the racetrack. Why were they in back, where the trainers and owners parked? She climbed out of the car and waited for her father to speak.

Mr. Griffen grabbed his wife's hand and smiled down at his children. He waited for a moment to draw out the suspense, then took a deep breath and spoke. "We've finally saved up enough money for Edgardale to purchase its own stallion. His name is Royal Renegade, and he's a racing stallion. He's running in the sixth race today."

"A racer!" Rory crowed. "Ashleigh, we're going to have a real racer!"

"Hold on just a minute," Mr. Griffen said, raising

his hands as everyone began to talk at once. "He's not ours yet. Renegade only has one race under his saddle, and the owner wanted to race the colt one more time before he sold him. We're still haggling over the price. But he seemed pretty anxious to sell."

"Do we get to see him now?" Ashleigh asked breathlessly. She looked across the way into the busy stable, where horses, grooms, and trainers went about their daily business of preparing for the races. Royal Renegade was there somewhere.

Mrs. Griffen tucked a lock of her blond hair back into place and herded everyone toward the security shack at the back gate. "Tom Rolland—that's Renegade's owner—is going to meet us at the gate and let us have a quick peek at the stallion before the race," she explained. "Then we'll go over to the front side and wait for the sixth race."

"Is it a big race?" Ashleigh asked.

Mr. Griffen nodded. "It's a stakes race for three-year-olds. Renegade finished third in a maiden allowance race his first outing. Mr. Rolland thought the colt ran well enough to enter him in a stakes race this time."

"Wow, Renegade is only three?" Ashleigh said.

Mrs. Griffen gave the security guard their name and waited for him to page Mr. Rolland. "Yes, and wait until you see him." She smiled. "He's a big, handsome bay with a full blaze and one white sock on his front right leg."

"Some of the horses in Renegade's race are con-tenders for the Kentucky Derby," Mr. Griffen said. "Fast Cat, from Golden Hills Farm, is one of them. The *Daily Racing Form* thinks he's the fastest three-year-old running this year."

"Royal Renegade." Ashleigh repeated the name in a whisper. She liked the way it rolled off her tongue. A horse with a name like that could definitely win the Kentucky Derby! "So is Renegade going to the Derby, too?" Ashleigh asked. If they bought Renegade, Edgar-dale wouldn't have to wait for one of their own foals to grow up and race. Renegade was the perfect age for the Derby right now.

Mr. Griffen shrugged. "I'm sure Mr. Rolland had him nominated at birth, but I don't think the colt has raced enough to know for sure. That's why we're trying to buy Renegade now. Once he starts living up to his pedigree, his price will go up, and we won't be able to afford him."

Mrs. Griffen nodded in agreement. "Mike Smith has had his eye on Renegade for quite a while. He alerted us when he found out Mr. Rolland was think-ing of selling him. The trick is to buy the colt now and prove him as a racer. That will make him worth a lot more money as a breeding stallion."

Ashleigh knew that a good stallion with a proven race history could be worth millions of dollars in stud fees. She couldn't believe Renegade might actually be theirs.

"I thought you said three is young for breeding." Caroline looked from her mother to her father.

"It is too young for a complete booking," Mr. Griffen agreed. "We'll only breed a few of our own mares and a couple of outsiders this season. We need to get a few foals on the ground so breeders can see the kind of foals Renegade can produce. Next year, when Renegade is four, we'll breed all of our own stock and a few more outside mares." He reached out to smooth the rooster tail on top of Rory's head. "When Renegade is five, we'll stand him to a full book of outside mares plus our own."

A stallion! Ashleigh thought as she kicked at the bits of gravel on the blacktop. *A racing stallion!* Her head spun in a dizzying circle. Two of her very best dreams were going to come true at the same time. Edgardale would finally have a stallion of its own. And if they were very lucky, Royal Renegade might even run in the Kentucky Derby!

2

"Can we help get Renegade ready for the race?" Ashleigh asked her parents.

Mrs. Griffen shook her head. "I doubt Mr. Rolland will need our help. He's got his own grooms, and the horse isn't ours yet, Ash."

"But he will be soon," Ashleigh said hopefully.

Mrs. Griffen peered down the first shed row. "I think that's Mr. Rolland." She pointed to a thin man with dark, slicked-back hair who strode purposefully down the aisle.

Ashleigh watched as Mr. Rolland approached. She grimaced as he smiled, showing a full set of yellowed teeth. He shook her father's hand and bowed at her mother—every inch the polite owner-trainer. Still, he gave Ashleigh the creeps.

Tom Rolland clapped. "Well, shall we go see the big new horse?"

Everyone nodded as they followed the skinny trainer to the stabling area. Bay, brown, gray, and chestnut Thoroughbreds poked their heads over stall doors as they passed. Grooms scurried about, raking shed rows or preparing lunch for their elegant charges. Ashleigh sighed happily. She loved coming to the racetrack!

"That's our new test barn up on the hill," Mr. Rolland said, pointing to a gray concrete building with a green roof. "Over there are the four new barns to match it."

"How many horses are here?" Ashleigh asked, admiring the long-legged horses cooling out on hot walkers between barns.

"There's stalls for four hundred horses," Tom Rolland said.

"Wow!" Ashleigh poked her little brother. "Can you imagine—four hundred Thoroughbreds?"

"Yes!" Rory answered with a big smile. "But when do we get to see *our* horse?"

Mrs. Griffen gave Rory a warning glance. "Renegade isn't *our* horse yet, Rory. We still have to settle on a price with Mr. Rolland."

"But he will be ours," Rory protested. "We'll give him a good home."

"I'm sure you will, little guy," Mr. Rolland said in his high, squeaky voice. He reached out to pat Rory on the head.

Ashleigh saw her little brother shrink from the man's touch. She was glad to see she wasn't the only one who thought Mr. Rolland was creepy.

"Here we are." The trainer gestured toward his shed row.

Ashleigh stared down the length of the aisle. The other barns had neatly swept shed rows with curtains in their racing colors, houseplants, neat leather halters, and shiny brass nameplates. But Tom Rolland's barn was messy and drab. Bits of straw were scattered everywhere, and a few piles of manure lay underfoot.

Ashleigh peeked into one of the stalls. The stall had been mucked, but not with much care. Pieces of wet, dirty straw were strewn here and there, and the chestnut that occupied the stall looked like he hadn't been groomed. The dried sweat from a previous workout still clung to the horse's coat.

If this was the way Mr. Rolland kept his barn, they had better get Renegade to Edgardale as soon as possible!

"Johnny, grab Renegade out of the stall for me. We've got prospective clients here to see him," Mr. Rolland said.

Ashleigh stared at the unshaven man who grabbed an old nylon halter off its peg and went into the stall nearest the tack room. She sucked in her breath when

Royal Renegade was led from his stall. The bay stallion stepped regally into the aisle with his head held high. "He's beautiful!" Ashleigh said in awe. She stepped around to his head, and Renegade poked his white nose into her shoulder, woofing softly into her hair.

"Get back, Renegade!" Mr. Rolland commanded sharply. He grabbed the lead rope out of Johnny's hand and jerked hard on the lead shank, snapping the stallion painfully across the bridge of his soft nose. Renegade snorted and quickly backed off, eyeing the trainer suspiciously.

"He didn't do anything wrong!" Ashleigh said in Renegade's defense. "He was just trying to be friendly." Ashleigh caught the warning look from her father, telling her not to press the matter further. But she also noted the disapproving frown her mother gave Mr. Rolland.

"Maybe we'd better put the colt back in his stall," Mr. Griffen suggested.

Tom Rolland jerked the lead rope once more and handed it back to Johnny, who put Renegade back into his stall. "You never can be too careful with these stallions. You've got to show them who's boss." He chuckled, running his hand through his greasy hair.

Ashleigh was so furious, she could have kicked the man. Renegade had seemed perfectly well mannered.

But the creepy trainer had punished the colt for trying to make friends.

"Come on into the tack room and I'll pour you a cup of coffee," Mr. Rolland said to the adults.

As her parents stepped into the tack room, Ashleigh moved quickly to Renegade's stall.

"I don't know, Ash. Maybe you'd better not," Caroline warned.

Rory watched the tack-room door warily, obviously frightened of Mr. Rolland.

"Renegade's not mean," Ashleigh said. "You can tell by his eyes." She admired the stallion's kind, brown eyes, which peered out at Ashleigh from the corner of his stall. "Come on, pretty boy," Ashleigh crooned. "I won't hurt you." She stuck her hand into the stall, palm up, and continued to talk to the wary horse.

Renegade flicked his ears at the sound of Ashleigh's voice, seeming to weigh his choices. After a moment he tossed his head and stepped forward, thrusting his muzzle into Ashleigh's hand.

Ashleigh smiled as Renegade lipped the collar of her coat and nuzzled her hair. She was cautious, knowing that stallions *did* like to bite, but she didn't think Renegade would hurt her. She ran her hand down his blaze and marveled at the sleek feel of his coat. Mr. Rolland had known they were coming to see

Renegade, so he had probably done a good job of brushing him for once, Ashleigh thought angrily.

"Here they come," Rory whispered.

Ashleigh stepped back from the stall. She didn't want Renegade getting into trouble again because of her.

"Let's head up to the cafeteria and grab a quick snack, then go over to the front side," Mrs. Griffen suggested.

Ashleigh waited until they were seated in the horsemen's cafeteria before she voiced her opinion. "I think we need to get Renegade out of there quick before Mr. Rolland wrecks him."

"Yeah," Rory agreed, chewing a large bite of peanut-butter-and-jelly sandwich.

Even Caroline nodded.

Mr. Griffen poured some cream into his coffee, then offered it to his wife. "I agree with you, Ash. Mr. Rolland doesn't take very good care of his stock. But he's got his price, and it's a bit high for us. I'm not sure if we can settle on terms that we both agree on."

Ashleigh toyed with her sandwich. Mr. Rolland had to bring down his price! She waited for her family to finish eating before they headed to the front side of the racetrack.

Despite the cool weather and leafless trees, Turfway

Park was beautiful. There was a lake in the center of the track, bordered by a neat hedge, and pretty evergreen trees towered up here and there along the fence line. At the far end of the track was a white-fenced ring where show jumping took place in the warmer months.

Sleek Thoroughbreds and their grooms and trainers were heading across the track to the front side for the first race of the day. Ashleigh's mother and father took a table in the clubhouse and purchased a program.

After they sat down, Ashleigh peeked over her parents' shoulders at the card for Renegade's race. The handicapper for the program had Renegade picked to run sixth. Ashleigh hoped he did better than that. If they were going to stand Renegade to outside mares and sell his babies through auction, he'd need to have a pretty impressive race record.

Ashleigh got permission to take Rory with her to stand down at the rail while Caroline and her parents remained at their table. Caroline couldn't understand standing out in the cool air when they had a perfectly good view from their warm clubhouse seats. But Ashleigh and Rory knew better—they wanted to get as close to the horses as they could.

"How much longer do we have?" Rory asked as another batch of horses entered the walking ring.

"Renegade is in the next race," Ashleigh said, scanning the back fence to see if she could catch a glimpse of the large bay. But she knew Mr. Rolland would probably leave Renegade in his stall until the last minute to avoid overexciting him.

When Renegade's race came, Ashleigh and Rory crowded up close to the walking ring and saddling paddock so they could get a good view of the horse. Ashleigh felt a hand on her shoulder and turned to see the rest of her family behind her.

"Here he comes," Mrs. Griffen said, pointing at the pony rider who was just handing Renegade off to Mr. Rolland's groom. The creepy trainer walked several steps behind his horse.

"He looks sharp," Mr. Griffen commented as he eyed the other horses in the ring. "But Renegade's going to have to give it his best shot if he's going to get a piece of this race. There are some really tough horses running."

Mr. Rolland motioned for Johnny to bring the colt in to be saddled. Renegade stood like a gentleman, but he chomped at the bit and blew through his lips several times, indicating his readiness to be off.

"There's the call to the post!" Caroline said.

"Let's hurry back to our seats." Mr. Griffen took his wife's hand. "Ashleigh, I assume you and Rory are going to watch the race from your usual place?"

Ashleigh nodded, then grabbed Rory and cut through the crowd to reach her favorite spot on the rail. She couldn't take her eyes off Renegade as he pranced in the post parade, arching his neck and snorting. "You'll show them, boy," Ashleigh shouted as Renegade and his jockey rode past.

Renegade's jockey, a veteran rider named Mark Tremel, looked down at her and smiled. He gave the thumbs-up sign and then asked the colt for a jog, heading for the gate, which was parked at the mile-and-an-eighth marker. Ashleigh grinned excitedly. Someday that was going to be her up in the jockey's saddle!

"The horses are now loading into the starting gate for today's feature race," the announcer called.

"Get ready," Ashleigh said, lifting Rory up so he could see better. "Renegade's jockey is wearing purple silks. Watch for the purple colors when they break out of the gate."

"Royal Renegade, the number-four horse, is loaded in," the announcer said. "The number-five horse, Lively Notion, is acting up behind the gate."

With the gate only a furlong, or an eighth of a mile, up the track, Ashleigh could see most of what was happening. The gate crew finally got Lively Notion loaded, but he fussed the whole time until the bell sounded.

"They're running!" the announcer shouted.

"Oh, no!" Ashleigh cried as Lively Notion came out sideways, knocking into Renegade. She gasped as the bay stallion floundered on the track, trying to get his feet under him. By the time he got his balance and began to run, the rest of the field had him trapped on the inside rail at the back of the pack.

"Looks like he's in trouble," Rory said with a worried frown.

Ashleigh bit her lip as the horses pounded around the clubhouse turn and she lost sight of Renegade for the moment. She listened to the announcer's call, waiting to hear Renegade's name, but he never said it.

"He's moving up a little," Rory said as he pointed to the purple blur going into the last turn.

"Royal Renegade moves steadily on the outside behind Sure Goal," the announcer finally called. "Fast Cat is in first, and Sam's Girl is being challenged for second by Noble Event."

"Come on, Renegade." Ashleigh spoke under her breath as she watched the bay stallion move up another notch.

"They're coming around the final turn, and Royal Renegade has moved into fifth," the announcer said. "Fast Cat retains his lead, but Noble Event has moved into second place."

Ashleigh watched as the jockey swung Renegade wide on the final turn, taking him out to where the footing was better. "He's moving up!" Ashleigh screamed. "Come on, Renegade!"

Ashleigh stopped breathing altogether as she watched Renegade lengthen his stride and attempt to catch the leaders. Not only was the big bay beautiful to look at, but he also had heart.

"Royal Renegade moves into fourth place with his eye on the leader," the announcer yelled.

"Come on, Renegade!" Rory and Ashleigh screamed, pounding the fence. But there wasn't enough time to catch the leader. Fast Cat crossed the wire first, with Noble Event a nose behind him.

"Royal Renegade finishes third!" the announcer called. "Please hold all tickets until the results are final."

Ashleigh grabbed Rory and pushed her way over to where the jockeys would return with their tired mounts to be unsaddled. A moment later her parents and Caroline joined them.

Ashleigh frowned. "He could have won that race if he hadn't been bumped."

Mr. Griffen ran a hand through his hair. "I think he ran a heck of a race, all things considered," he said. "Especially since he wasn't even expected to place."

Mrs. Griffen nodded. "I think he's the horse for us."

Renegade trotted back to the finish line, his sides heaving and his nostrils extended to show their delicate pink lining. His jockey flipped his whip at the track stewards to indicate that there was no foul.

"Why isn't he calling a foul after he got hit so hard coming out of the gate?" Caroline asked.

"None of the horses that beat him were involved in the incident," Ashleigh explained. "It wouldn't do any good to call the foul."

"Look." Mrs. Griffen pointed to where they were unsaddling Renegade. "Mr. Rolland is motioning for us to follow him back to the barn."

Mr. Griffen rounded everyone up and ushered them through the security gap to follow Renegade as he was led back to the barn. "I guess it's time to buy a racehorse," he said with a tight smile. "Let's hope Mr. Rolland wasn't so impressed with the race that he ups his price."

Ashleigh shoved her hands deep into her pockets as they followed Mr. Rolland to the stables. She eyed the man suspiciously. It would be just like Mr. Rolland to suddenly up Renegade's price so high, the Griffens could never afford him. Ashleigh didn't trust the owner-trainer at all.

They reached the barn, and Ashleigh sat with her brother and sister on a bale of straw while their parents went into the tack room to talk things over with Mr. Rolland. Johnny bathed Renegade and then hooked him onto the hot walker to cool out.

After several minutes the door to the tack room creaked open, and Ashleigh's head snapped in that direction. Her parents looked a little irritated as they stepped into the aisleway.

"Let's go, kids," Mr. Griffen said in a measured voice as he settled his hat firmly on his head.

"Did you—" Ashleigh cut the question short at a stern look from her mother. *Oh, no,* Ashleigh thought worriedly as she hurried down the shed row with the rest of her family.

"What happened?" Caroline asked when they were out of Mr. Rolland's hearing.

Mrs. Griffen sighed. "Our offer wasn't good enough."

"Hmmph!" Mr. Griffen snorted. "The offer was perfectly acceptable to him the last time we spoke." They reached the car, and he flipped his key ring out of his pocket, jamming the car key into the door lock. "He wants more money now, and we just don't have the funds to pay his asking price."

Ashleigh felt a hollow in the pit of her stomach. The deal was off. Edgardale wouldn't be getting the stallion. She thought of Mr. Rolland's messy stalls and the ungroomed horses and the horrible way he treated the stallion. Ashleigh felt sick to her stomach.

"Royal Renegade isn't coming to live with us?" Rory asked in a small voice.

Mrs. Griffen patted Rory's cheek as she buckled him into the backseat of the car. "No, honey. Renegade will be staying here with Mr. Rolland."

Everyone settled into the car and sat in stony silence. They had been so close, and Renegade would have been perfect for Edgardale!

Mr. Griffen started the car and exited the parking lot.

"Mr. and Mrs. Griffen!"

Everyone turned at the sound of the loud, high-pitched voice. Mr. Rolland was standing in the middle of the roadway, waving his arms.

"Just a minute, please," the trainer hollered as he jogged toward them. He was out of breath by the time he reached the car and poked his head through the open front window. "I'm glad I caught you," he huffed. "I've decided to accept your offer. I'll bring the colt by tomorrow afternoon. You have your check ready, and I'll bring his papers."

The skinny man nodded briskly, then turned and walked off, leaving everyone in the car in stunned silence.

Ashleigh stared suspiciously at the man's retreating form. Even though she desperately wanted Renegade for Edgardale, she could understand why Mr. Rolland would up his price after the great race the colt had run. But why would he suddenly change his mind and accept their offer?

Elaine Griffen looked around the car in disbelief. "Well, then, I guess we did just buy ourselves a horse after all."

"Yes!" Ashleigh cried. She pumped her fist in the air, deciding to cast aside her suspicions about the shady trainer. It really didn't matter what made him change his mind, she decided. The important thing was that he had, and Renegade was coming to live at Edgardale!

3

Ashleigh rose early the next morning. She pulled on her jeans and joined her mother for a quick bowl of cereal, then went to the barn to start her chores. Her father had gotten up early to meet Dr. Frankel for Renegade's vet check. She felt a tingle of excitement race up her spine as she entered the barn. Today Edgardale would get its very own stallion!

She stopped by Stardust's stall. "Hey, girl," Ashleigh called over the stall door to the chestnut mare. She laughed when Stardust nickered a greeting from the bottom of the bucket, refusing to pull out her head until every last oat was licked clean. "You're such a clown!" Ashleigh giggled. "We'll go for a quick ride with Mona when my stalls are done. I can't wait to tell her—Edgardale is getting a handsome bay stallion."

Ashleigh knew the mare couldn't understand what she was saying, but Stardust definitely sensed Ashleigh's excited mood. She bobbed her head and blew through her lips before going back to munching her oats.

Ashleigh picked up the muck rake and began forking dirty bedding into the wheelbarrow. She had overheard Jonas telling her mother that Marvy Mary and Jolita had been put in the foaling stalls last night. New foals and warmer weather were the best parts of spring, Ashleigh thought. And by next year Renegade would have his first foals on the ground.

She finished her stalls while her mother prepared the big box stall and adjoining paddock at the end of the barn for the new stud. Like most breeding farms, Edgardale had a special stall built to house a breeding stallion. The paddock fences were higher than normal to prevent the stud from jumping out to get at the mares, and there was a strand of electric wire along the top board to discourage an aggressive stallion from pressing against the rails.

Ashleigh didn't think they had to worry about Renegade misbehaving, but it was better to take precautions just in case.

Mr. Griffen pulled into the driveway just as Ashleigh was finishing her chores.

Mrs. Griffen motioned to Ashleigh. "Let's go see what the vet had to say."

Ashleigh took a deep breath. If Dr. Frankel had

found anything wrong during the vet check, the deal would be off. Renegade wouldn't come to Edgardale to race or to stand at stud. She felt herself relax when her father stepped from the car with a big smile on his face.

"Everything went well," Mr. Griffen assured them. "Dr. Frankel went over the colt from nose to hoof, and the only thing he found wrong was a small scar on Renegade's front pastern. All the x rays came back clean, too."

Ashleigh wrapped her arms around herself and grinned. Renegade had passed the final hurdle. He would be theirs within hours!

Ashleigh asked permission to ride Stardust over to Mona's to deliver the good news.

"Can I go with you on Moe?" Rory pleaded.

Mrs. Griffen turned to Ashleigh. "Feel like having a sidekick this morning?"

Ashleigh couldn't resist her little brother's hopeful look. "Sure. Just hurry up and get Moe saddled. We don't have much time before Renegade comes." She laughed at the look of sheer joy on her little brother's face. He felt the same way about riding as she did. "Don't forget your helmet!" she called after his departing form.

By the time she had Stardust saddled, Rory was ready to go.

"Can we race down the driveway?" Rory asked as he mounted the little brown pony.

Ashleigh shook her head. "You know you've got to warm your horse up before you do any fast work," she scolded. "Besides, remember what happened that time I tried racing Moe against Mona's big Thoroughbred mare?"

Rory's face took on a serious expression as he nodded solemnly. "I don't want Moe to get hurt again."

"Good," Ashleigh said. "Let's ask our horses for a trot down the driveway. Then we can canter a little in the field on the way to Mona's house."

Mona was just finishing her morning chores when they trotted into the stable yard.

"Uh-oh." Mona looked at Ashleigh with a questioning gaze. "Did we have plans to go riding this morning?"

"No, this is a surprise visit," Ashleigh said with a smile. She dismounted and hooked Stardust into the crossties in the Gardeners' barn, then led Rory over to the big arena so he could ride while she and Mona talked. "Guess who's coming to Edgardale today?" she asked her friend.

"Knowing you, it could be anyone," Mona teased, wrinkling her freckly nose. "But I'm guessing it must be a horse."

Ashleigh nodded.

Mona looked surprised. "Your parents bought you a Thoroughbred?"

"Well, he's not exactly for me." Ashleigh grinned. "Edgardale bought a racing stallion! My parents want to run him a few more times so he can establish a good record, then we're going to retire him to stud. We just watched him race yesterday. His name is Royal Renegade, and he's amazing!"

"Is he at your place right now?" Mona asked hopefully.

"No, but he's going to be delivered soon," Ashleigh said. "Want to come over and wait with me?"

"You bet!" Mona clapped. "Let me go get Frisky." She ran to the barn, grabbing a halter from the wall and calling for her mare. She was back in a few minutes with nothing but a bridle on the bay mare.

"You're going to ride bareback?" Ashleigh looked skeptical as she watched her friend mount the feisty mare. Frisky always managed to live up to her name.

Mona shimmied into place on Frisky's back and steadied the mare's reins. "I didn't want to waste time with the saddle. I want to be there when your new horse shows up. Call Rory, and let's get going. You can give me all the details on the way back to Edgardale."

The three of them trotted across the field toward the Griffen farm. A loud rattle from down the road drew their attention. They turned to see a beat-up horse trailer making its way slowly down the road.

Mona pulled Frisky to a halt. "That couldn't be Renegade, could it?" she asked in disbelief. "You said your parents paid a lot of money for him. That trailer looks like it's ready for the junkyard."

Ashleigh pulled Stardust alongside Mona's mare and raised her hand to shield her eyes. "If you knew how creepy the owner was, you wouldn't be surprised."

They waited until the trailer passed, then pulled their horses in behind it and trotted back to Edgardale. "Be careful, Rory," Ashleigh warned. "You know Moe always likes to go fast when he's heading for home."

They arrived in the stable yard just as Renegade was being unloaded. The large, well-muscled bay stallion backed out of the trailer and stood with his head held high, surveying his new home.

"He's beautiful!" Mona said in awe.

Ashleigh smiled and jumped down from her horse. "What do you think, Stardust? He's a handsome devil, isn't he?"

As if Stardust understood the question, the little chestnut mare let out a loud welcoming whinny.

Renegade's head snapped around to look at them, and he nickered a greeting.

"Whoa!" Rory cried in surprise as Moe tossed his head and tried to bolt forward to greet the new horse.

Ashleigh reached out to steady Moe's reins. "Hold him tight, Rory. Renegade might not be as happy to see Moe as Moe is to meet him."

Ashleigh frowned when Mr. Rolland started in with his hard-handed method of handling the stallion, yanking on the lead shank and barking out commands. Renegade was behaving perfectly well—he didn't deserve such mean treatment.

"Here, let me take him." Mr. Griffen stepped forward, taking the lead rope from Mr. Rolland's hands. "Elaine, could you open Renegade's stall for me? Ashleigh, you kids can tie your horses in their stalls for now."

Elaine Griffen ran ahead, opening the stall door for her husband. When Renegade was inside, they turned him loose and watched as he sniffed the bedding, snorting at his new surroundings. At the sound of a distant neigh Renegade trotted out of the stall to inspect his new paddock.

Caroline and Jonas arrived. Jonas let out a slow whistle. "That's one nice horse," he said in admiration. "So this is the stallion we stayed up all those nights researching?" He studied Renegade's clean lines and proud demeanor. "You were right, Mrs. G. This horse is going to do Edgardale proud. He looks just as good as his pedigree says he should."

"Well, he's not officially yours yet," Mr. Rolland

said in his squeaky voice, tapping the registration papers against his palm.

Ashleigh shot him a suspicious look. *What was the strange man up to now?* she wondered.

Mr. Griffen cleared his throat and rubbed his chin. "You're not trying to raise the price on us again, are you, Mr. Rolland?" He leveled his gaze at the trainer. "We did have a gentlemen's agreement on this."

"Of course." Mr. Rolland put his hands in the air. "I was just pulling your leg. I've already signed over the papers. All I need is your cashier's check."

Mrs. Griffen directed Mr. Rolland into the barn office so they could complete the transaction. Five minutes later Mr. Rolland walked quickly back to his beat-up trailer, check in hand.

Ashleigh turned to her parents. "Is that it? Is he really ours?" She felt a poke at her shoulder and a soft tug on her shirtsleeve as Renegade extended his neck over the stall door, trying to get her attention.

"He's all ours," Mrs. Griffen said, beaming at the big, handsome horse.

Ashleigh gazed up at Renegade and ran her hand down his long, white blaze. "You're really ours," she said in disbelief. Edgardale finally had a stallion of its own, and he was the most perfect stallion imaginable, better than any horse Ashleigh had ever dreamed of.

4

"When will Renegade start his training?" Ashleigh asked as she watched the proud stallion circle his paddock, inspecting every inch of it.

Mr. Griffen leaned against the stall door, chewing on a stem of hay. "Renegade won't get any time off. He'll get today to rest and settle in, then we'll start him back in training tomorrow. Dr. Frankel said the colt's cleared to start breeding a few mares, too," Mr. Griffen explained. "Daniel Carter will bring one of his mares over this week, and we've got a couple of our own ready to breed."

"Wow, that's awfully quick," Ashleigh remarked.

Mr. Griffen nodded. "We're a breeding farm, Ashleigh. It's March, and that's the optimum time for Thoroughbreds if you want early foals on the ground." He ruffled Ashleigh's hair and smiled. "You know those buyers at the sale like the early colts because they're bigger and stronger."

Ashleigh nodded. She knew that people who ran their horses as two-year-olds or early three-year-olds liked the ones that were born as close to January 1 as possible since that was the birthday of all Thoroughbreds, according to The Jockey Club, no matter when they were born. Because they were more mature, they had a distinct advantage over the racers that were born later in the year. Once they reached their fourth year, things seemed to level out and the age difference didn't make as much difference.

Mr. Griffen looked out at the stallion thoughtfully. "Besides, we've put all of our extra money into that guy. We can't afford to breed to any outside studs this year. Our mares have got to be bred to Renegade. The sooner he starts producing, the sooner we'll be out of debt."

Ashleigh looked up in concern. She knew money was always a little tight at Edgardale. Her parents were trying to build the operation up slowly, but to get ahead, they always had to spend beyond their means.

Mr. Griffen smiled at Ashleigh. "Don't worry, kiddo. As soon as we build up Renegade's race record and get a few foals on the ground, we'll be fine. Do you want to help with Renegade's training? Mike and

Rhoda will be here when you get home from school tomorrow."

Ashleigh looked up in surprise. "Mike and Rhoda are coming?" She hadn't seen Rhoda for several months. Rhoda was her favorite jockey, and Ashleigh hoped to be just like her when she grew up.

Mrs. Griffen chuckled as she joined them at the stall door. "You didn't think we'd take on a big project like training Renegade on our own, did you? Your father and I are good at the breeding end of it, but we're going to need a great trainer like Mike and an experienced jockey like Rhoda to help Renegade win races. The Wortons have offered us the use of their training track, so we'll be able to keep Renegade right here at Edgardale."

Ashleigh always learned so much from the petite jockey and the stocky trainer. She hurried up to the house. She had a book report to finish by Tuesday and some math problems to tackle. She wanted to make sure all of her homework was finished before Mike and Rhoda arrived.

"Good to see you again, Ashleigh!" Rhoda Kat called as she walked into the barn on Monday afternoon. "It looks like I'll be coming down in the afternoons during the week to gallop your new horse. Mike tells me you and Stardust are getting pretty good at ponying, so you'll be handling Renegade's exercise program between my gallops."

Ashleigh gaped at Rhoda. Mike and her parents came up behind her. "Really?" she asked them. "Do I really get to pony Renegade?"

Mr. Griffen chuckled. "Well, that depends on how Renegade behaves himself today. And how well he and Stardust get along. Why don't you saddle up Stardust now? You can pony Rhoda and Renegade over to the Wortons' track."

Mrs. Griffen handed Ashleigh her helmet. "From everything we've seen, Renegade is really easy to handle. But never forget that he's a stallion," she warned. "If he starts misbehaving, I'll have to take over the ponying for you."

"You're so lucky!" Rory said as he helped Ashleigh get her tack.

Ashleigh hooked Stardust into the crossties and ran a body brush quickly over the mare's copper coat. "Yeah, but I'm also really nervous," she admitted. "This is a big responsibility. What if I goof up?"

Caroline pushed the wheelbarrow to her next stall. She rolled her eyes. "Come on, Ash. You did fine with all those hots you ponied for Mike a while back. I know you can do this. Besides, Rhoda will be riding Renegade. She'll keep him under control."

Ashleigh smiled and took a deep breath, letting it out slowly. "You're right. We'll be fine, won't we, Stardust?" She pulled the girth snug on her saddle and plopped her helmet into place. "I'm going to warm Stardust up in the paddock."

"Do you think she needs it?" Caroline asked as she forked some dirty bedding into the wheelbarrow.

Ashleigh unsnapped her mare from the crossties. "It's hard enough trying to hang on to a racer when your horse is behaving perfectly. It's almost impossible to do when your pony horse thinks she's in a rodeo!"

Caroline's laughter echoed behind her as Ashleigh left the barn, heading for the large paddock out front.

Ashleigh closed the gate and mounted up. "Let's make sure we wear you down a little before we take on Renegade," she told Stardust. "I don't want you beating him to the finish line!"

Ashleigh trotted Stardust several times around the large paddock before breaking her into a canter. Stardust perked her ears and strained at the bit, but Ashleigh held her steady, circling the paddock several more times until she felt the mare relax. After another large circle she pulled her mare to a walk and returned to the barn. Renegade was saddled and Rhoda was just mounting up when they arrived back at the stable yard.

"Are you ready, Ash?" Mrs. Griffen said, leading Renegade over to where Ashleigh and Stardust were waiting.

Ashleigh nodded, feeling her heart rate jump as Renegade began to prance and chomp at the bit.

Rhoda saw the look of worry on Ashleigh's face and smiled encouragingly. "You'll do fine, Ash. Just relax and take a good hold of him. He's a big colt, but he seems pretty well mannered."

Ashleigh smiled, feeling her lips stick to her teeth. She hadn't expected to be this nervous. She remembered what her mother and father had told her about a horse being able to sense a person's fear, so she forced herself to relax.

"Just put your pony rope through the ring on his bit. He'll be fine," Rhoda assured her.

As Rhoda and Renegade pulled alongside them, Ashleigh leaned over and ran the leather lead through Renegade's bit. The big horse rubbed his head on her shoulder, almost knocking Ashleigh out of the saddle.

"Careful there," Rhoda warned.

Ashleigh straightened up. "It's okay. He was just trying to scratch his head."

Renegade bumped his shoulder into Stardust, and the little mare pinned her ears, giving the big colt a warning with a flick of her tail. Ashleigh tugged on her reins, cautioning Stardust against doing anything foolish. After a few minutes on the trail they arrived at the Wortons' training track. Her family and Mike had driven the car over and were waiting for them when they arrived.

Mike stepped up to the track, leaning his elbows on the white boards of the rail. "Ashleigh, I want you to backtrack Renegade at a walk, then turn around and break the horses into a trot. When Rhoda says she's ready, turn them loose."

Ashleigh nodded, grabbing a steady hold on Renegade, who was beginning to dance and toss his head. "Easy, big guy," Ashleigh said, giving a little tug on the line. To her relief, Renegade immediately settled back down to a walk.

"Rhoda," Mike called. "Once you're let loose, I want you to give him two easy laps around the track at a slow canter. If he's handling okay, you can pick up a little speed on your last half mile."

Ashleigh put all of her concentration into her work. She didn't want to blow this. She stopped the horses and turned them in toward the inside rail, just like she had seen the jockeys at the racetrack do. They stood for a few moments until both horses were quiet, then turned and started up the track.

"Let's put them into a slow trot," Rhoda instructed. "Give me a little more line on the lead rope. I need to get control of his head so I can feel how easy his mouth is."

Ashleigh took a deep breath and asked Stardust for a slow trot, letting another six inches of line pass through her fingers. The horses stepped out in unison, moving quietly down the track.

Rhoda posted to the motion of the big colt, then stood in the stirrups and crossed the reins just above Renegade's withers, leaning into her hold and preparing for the coming gallop. "Stay with me until we hit the next eighth pole, then you can turn me loose, Ash."

Ashleigh nodded. A big smile tugged at the corners of her mouth, and she couldn't help but grin. Rhoda was a great jockey. It was so cool to be able to work with her this closely. Ashleigh watched every move the young jockey made, storing all the information for the day she would get to gallop her first Thoroughbred on a real racetrack.

"Okay," Rhoda said when they reached the gap in the track where Mike and the Griffens stood. "We're doing fine. Turn us loose."

Ashleigh let go of one end of the pony rope, letting

it slide through the ring of the bit. When the rope was clear, she pulled Stardust up and watched as Rhoda broke Renegade into a slow canter. She walked Stardust off the track to stand by her parents. When Renegade was making his last lap, she would take Stardust to the end of the backstretch to pick them up and walk them back to the barn.

Mike watched Renegade as he moved into the top turn. "Looks like he's got power," he remarked. "He's moving well, but he's pulling at the bit. Rhoda looks like she's working hard to hold him back."

By the time Renegade passed by them for his second trip around the track, he had picked up a lot of speed. Rhoda was pulling hard on the reins, and the big colt's neck was bowed. Ashleigh could hear the colt puffing big breaths of air as he breezed by them.

"Get ahold of him, Rhoda!" Mike hollered from the sidelines. "He's working much faster than I wanted."

Rhoda's face was red from the strain of holding the big colt in when he wanted to run. She hunched her shoulders helplessly as she continued to fight the fast-galloping stallion.

"Better get Stardust down to the head of that turn," Mrs. Griffen said to Ashleigh. "It looks like Rhoda might have trouble pulling him up. Stand your mare in the center of the track. That should get Renegade's attention and help Rhoda bring him back under control."

Ashleigh kept her eye on the bay colt as she trotted Stardust down the track. Rhoda stood in her irons as they came up the back side. Renegade moved toward the center of the track, slowing his pace as he closed the distance between them. Rhoda smiled when he finally broke into a trot.

"Whew!" Rhoda said, wiping the sweat from her brow. "This is quite a horse! I wasn't sure if he was going to stop, but he knows the routine. He just likes pulling really strong when he's out there working." She reached down and patted the bay's sweaty neck.

Ashleigh ran her ponying line through Renegade's bit and walked them back toward the track gate.

"What do you think?" Mr. Griffen said as he followed them off the track.

Rhoda smiled broadly. "He's a real steamroller! This colt feels as good as any of the big stakes winners that I'm riding right now. Have you considered putting him in the Spiral Stakes?"

Ashleigh sucked in her breath. The Spiral Stakes was the first major Triple Crown prep race in the state of Kentucky. The mile-and-an-eighth stakes was the kickoff race for Derby season.

The trainer shrugged his broad shoulders. "I want to be sure of what we've got before I go entering him in those big races. I've got a race picked out for next week. You can breeze Renegade a couple of days before that race and see how he does. Ashleigh can pony him one day, then you'll come on Wednesday and we'll put a good breeze into him."

Rhoda nodded. "I'll see you back at the barn."

Ashleigh and Rhoda walked the horses back to Edgardale. Ashleigh hung on to every word the jockey had to say about Renegade. She wanted to ask Rhoda if she thought the colt might be Derby material, but she decided to wait until after Rhoda had ridden him in a few more gallops to ask her.

When they reached the barn, Rhoda hopped down and pulled the tack from Renegade's back.

"See you in a few days, boy," she told the stallion, patting his sweaty neck.

Ashleigh waved good-bye to Mike and Rhoda, then went to help her parents with Renegade. They were just starting his warm water bath.

"Can I help?" she asked.

Mrs. Griffen nodded. "Hand me the scraper and get his cooler. Jonas will walk him out, then hook him in the crossties for you to groom before he goes back in his stall."

Ashleigh was thrilled that her parents were letting her take part in Renegade's training. She ran for the cooler and readied the brush box while Jonas walked the colt out. She was going to make sure Renegade's coat gleamed when she was through. Renegade would never, ever look like those other horses in Mr. Rolland's stable, with dried sweat clinging to their dull coats, she promised herself.

"Here you go, Ash," Jonas said fifteen minutes later when he snapped Renegade into the crossties.

Ashleigh grabbed a low stool to stand on so she could reach Renegade's back and the top of his head. At first she was worried the big bay would fuss, but Renegade behaved perfectly, lowering his head and sighing contentedly as Ashleigh ran a series of curry-combs and soft brushes over his body.

Ashleigh's fingers passed over a rough spot on the back of Renegade's right front pastern. *This must be the scar Dr. Frankel found in the vet check,* Ashleigh thought. She wondered how he had gotten it—barbed wire, maybe? A trailer accident? She continued brushing, studying every inch of the stallion's body. The only other mark she found was a small lock of white hair in the middle of his black mane. Otherwise the stallion was perfect. The way Mr. Rolland treated his horses, it was amazing Renegade didn't have other scars.

Ashleigh's parents and Jonas were talking down at the end of the aisle. She knew it was rude to eavesdrop, but she couldn't resist when she heard Renegade's name mentioned.

"But that's a Derby prep race!" Jonas said. He sounded shocked.

Mr. Griffen's deep voice answered. "Yes, but I don't want to get ahead of ourselves. Let's just wait and see how the colt runs this week."

Ashleigh's heart pounded in her chest. Was there really a chance that Renegade would run in the Spiral Stakes? Renegade might even run in the Derby. She put down her brushes and stood back to admire the big bay stallion. He had the deep chest and strong hindquarters of a good runner. But did he have the heart of a Kentucky Derby winner? *He just might,* Ashleigh thought. She knew it was a long shot. So many good horses never even made it past the Derby prep races. But she could always dream.

Ashleigh put away the brushes and unsnapped Renegade from the crossties. She turned the stallion loose in his stall and watched him trot out into the connecting paddock. Renegade arched his neck and trumpeted to the mares, pricking his ears to listen to their answering calls. He tossed his elegant head and pranced around the paddock, his muscles rippling magnificently.

Ashleigh leaned against the stall door to watch the stallion. Her instincts told her that Renegade was special, but was he special enough to win races with the best horses in the country? Ashleigh crossed her fingers and closed her eyes for a moment, hoping for all the world that he was.

5

When Ashleigh arrived home from school on Tuesday, there was a strange truck and horse trailer parked in front of the barn. She recognized Daniel Carter, one of their neighbors from down the road, standing out in the stable yard, holding one of his broodmares.

Mrs. Griffen walked out of the barn with a chart in her hand. She waved to Ashleigh. "Mr. Carter's brought one of his mares to breed to Renegade. We're going to go ahead and cover her right now."

Ashleigh studied the mare. "Will it hurt Renegade's race training to be breeding mares?"

Mrs. Griffen shook her head. "Your father and Mike think that Renegade is so well behaved, he won't lose his cool." She pulled a tail wrap from her jacket pocket and began wrapping the mare's tail in preparation for breeding. "Of course, if the colt looks like he can't handle it mentally or physically, we'll hold off breeding for a month and concentrate on racing him before we give it another try."

Mr. Griffen stepped around the corner of the barn with Renegade's halter in his hand. "It's time to go to work," he called out to the stallion, who was quietly eating hay in his paddock. He lifted his head and eyed Mr. Griffen curiously as he approached.

"Oh, Ash, we've got a new foal," Mr. Griffen said, buckling the halter onto Renegade's head. "Marvy Mary had a nice filly this morning. They're still in the foaling stall if you want to take a look."

Ashleigh ran to the foaling stall, peeking in at the new bay filly that lay nestled in the straw. "She's beautiful!" Ashleigh whispered in awe. The tiny horse wobbled to her feet, staring up at Ashleigh inquisitively. Ashleigh could already tell the filly was going to be clever, just like her mother.

"You were running late for the bus this morning. I knew if I told you Marvy Mary was foaling, you'd miss it altogether."

Ashleigh giggled. "I would not!"

Mrs. Griffen gave her a mock frown and tapped her playfully on the head with the breeding chart. "If we let you stay home every time a mare foaled, you'd be graduating high school about the same time as your little brother," she teased.

Ashleigh took her place outside the breeding pen while her mother readied the mare. "Do you need the breeding hobbles?" Ashleigh asked.

Mr. Carter came up behind her and leaned against the railing. He shook his head. "No need. This old mare's a pro. She won't kick."

Ashleigh heard a shrill whinny and turned to see Renegade being walked through the gate of the corral. Since the stallion had never bred a mare before, Mr. Griffen took extra time with Renegade, letting him sniff noses with the mare and nicker to her.

The roan mare stood still until the stallion reached out to nip her shoulder. Ashleigh sucked in her breath as Mr. Carter's mare pinned her ears and wheeled, kicking out with a hind leg, catching Renegade square on the chest.

Renegade grunted and backed away, shaking his head and stomping his front leg to dispel the pain.

"Turn her away!" Mr. Griffen shouted as he pulled the stallion to the other side of the pen.

Jonas slipped through the gate, running to where Mr. Griffen stood with Renegade. "I'll hold his head while you check him out." Jonas huffed an exasperated breath and tsked. "I heard that hoof land all the way from the feed shed. Why weren't there any breeding hobbles on that mare?"

"My fault, my fault," Mr. Carter called, striding

over to examine Renegade, too. His whiskery face was creased with worry.

Mr. Griffen knelt in front of the big bay, running his hand over the stallion's chest. "I knew better," he said, shaking his head in disbelief. "I guess I just got anxious to get this guy producing foals." He stood and patted Renegade's neck. "He's seems okay," he told Mr. Carter. "Your old mare didn't have shoes on." He turned to Jonas. "We won't work him today, though."

"Are we done for now?" Mrs. Griffen asked.

Derek Griffen put his hands on his hips, looking back and forth between the mare and the stallion. "No, let's try it one more time. But this time we'll use the breeding hobbles."

Ashleigh watched as they strapped the mare's legs to prevent her from kicking. The hobbles looked uncomfortable, but the mare could still walk. Besides, one wrong kick could seriously injure or even kill a stallion. The hobbles were worth it, for Renegade's sake.

Ashleigh held her breath as Renegade approached the roan mare once more. The broodmare stood quietly, but Renegade was cautious, arching his neck and blowing heavily through his nostrils. The mare flicked her tail, and Renegade shied away, jumping to the side to prevent another kick.

"I'm going to try him again," Mr. Griffen said, gritting his teeth. He circled and led the bay toward the mare one more time. But Renegade turned away, disinterested. "Come on, big guy, we bought you to be a breeding stallion," Mr. Griffen said. He clucked at the stallion, but Renegade turned away, his ears pinned unhappily.

"What's the matter, Derek?" Mrs. Griffen asked.

Mr. Griffen sighed and led the bay colt from the pen. "I think he's had enough for now. We'll try him again after dinner."

They returned the horses to their stalls. Daniel Carter apologized for his mare's behavior, the men shook hands, and Mr. Carter drove away, promising to call the following day to see how things went.

Ashleigh hung around outside the tack-room door, raking the aisle and trying to listen to her parents' conversation.

"What are we going to do if he won't breed?" Mrs. Griffen asked, sounding worried.

Ashleigh leaned on the rake, waiting for her father's answer.

Mr. Griffen let out an exasperated sigh. "He's got to breed," he said. "We've paid a whole lot of money for that stallion. We don't even know if we could get our money back racing him. And what if he gets injured in a race or he can't run as well as we hoped . . . ? If

Renegade refuses to breed, we're in a lot of trouble."

Ashleigh felt her legs turn to jelly. *How much trouble?* she wondered. Was the farm in danger? She knew her parents had put every extra penny they had into buying the stallion. The tack-room door swung open, and Ashleigh ducked into an empty stall. She didn't want her parents to know she'd been eavesdropping.

Ashleigh waited until they had gone up to the house before she came out of the stall. It would be another hour until Caroline had supper ready. That meant it would be at least two hours before they would try breeding the mare again.

Ashleigh finished her meal before everyone else and asked to be excused to do her homework in the living room while the rest of the family finished their meal. Finally she heard her father say, "Okay, Elaine. Ready to try Renegade again?"

Mrs. Griffen gathered the dirty plates and put them in the sink. "You go on ahead and get started. I'll be down in just a minute. Ashleigh?"

It was her turn to do the dishes. Ashleigh rushed to the sink, frowning when she saw the stack of dirty plates. There was no way she could get them done in time to watch her parents breed Renegade.

Caroline nudged Ashleigh aside and rolled up her sleeves. "Go ahead, Ash. I know you're dying to. I'll switch with you, and you can do my dishes tomorrow night."

"Thanks, Caro, you're the best!" Ashleigh cried. She handed her sister the soapy sponge and raced for the door.

Caroline laughed. "Yeah, I'll remember you said that next time you're complaining about my nail polish smelling up the room."

When Ashleigh arrived, Mr. Griffen was just leading Renegade into the breeding pen, where Mrs. Griffen was holding Mr. Carter's mare. The roan mare turned her head and trumpeted a welcome whinny to the stallion.

Ashleigh smiled. This time everything was going to go right. Her father brought Renegade closer. The stallion pricked his ears at the mare's eager nicker, but then he planted his feet, refusing to walk forward any farther.

"Bring him around to her side and let him sniff noses with her. Maybe that will help," Jonas suggested from his place on the outside of the corral.

Renegade sniffed the mare and nickered to her, but he showed no interest in breeding.

"Maybe he just doesn't like this particular mare," Mrs. Griffen said. "Why don't we bring out My Georgina—she's ready to breed."

"I'll get her," Jonas volunteered. He turned to Ashleigh. "Can you handle Georgie's foal?"

Ashleigh nodded and ran after Jonas. They put a halter on both the mare and the foal and led them to the pen.

Mrs. Griffen stepped forward to take the lead rope from Ashleigh. "I'll take over from here, Ash. I don't want you in the pen with the stallion while we're breeding him. You might get hurt."

They went through the same routine with My Georgina. This time Renegade approached the big chestnut mare with more enthusiasm, nickering softly to her, but when it came time to breed the mare, the stallion turned away.

Mr. Griffen rubbed his hand over his eyes and sighed. "All right, we've had enough for one day. We'll try this again in the morning."

Ashleigh didn't like the look her parents exchanged. They put the mare and stallion back in their stalls, then went into the barn office. Ashleigh paid a quick visit to Stardust while she waited for them to come out. She heard the office door open and then her father's voice.

"We could be in a lot of trouble here, Elaine," Mr. Griffen said. "We've put a lot of money into this colt. He looks like he might turn out to be a decent racer, but we can't depend on him winning the big-money stakes. He's got to pull his weight here." He ran a hand nervously through his dark hair. "I don't know what we're going to do if he won't breed."

"Do you think we should sell him?" Mrs. Griffen asked. Ashleigh's heart sank to hear her even ask such a question.

Derek Griffen sighed and shook his head hopelessly. He turned out the barn lights and opened the door for his wife. "If he won't breed, we'll have to," Mr. Griffen said. "What good is a breeding stallion that won't breed? We're not set up to be a racing stable. We're only racing the colt to make him more valuable as a breeding stallion. I just hope it doesn't come to that."

Ashleigh sat in the dark, waiting for what she'd heard to settle in. Sell Renegade? They couldn't! She knew he was good enough to run in the Derby, and she was sure he could produce the kind of foals Edgardale would be proud of. She had to find a way to help Renegade!

6

Ashleigh hopped off the school bus on Wednesday afternoon and ran down the long driveway to Edgardale. Today she would pony Renegade all by herself. Even though the vet had given the colt the okay to be galloped, Mike had decided to give him a light work today, then Rhoda would work him on Thursday.

Ashleigh's mind wandered as she tossed her book bag onto her bed and reached for her jeans. If Renegade got in a few days of exercise, he might forget about the grouchy mare and change his mind about breeding her. She knew it was unusual for a stallion to be a shy breeder, but sometimes it happened. Dr. Frankel had reminded them that the great racehorse Secretariat had started out as a shy breeder. Ashleigh pursed her lips in determination. There had to be hope for Renegade!

Quickly she changed her clothes and hurried down to the barn. Her parents had the stallion out in the aisle and were grooming him.

"Gee, I thought maybe you'd get busy with your homework and forget about ponying Renegade today," Mrs. Griffen teased.

"No way!" Ashleigh laughed and grabbed the brush box, heading for Stardust's stall. "How's the new filly doing?" she asked when she noticed that Marvy Mary and her new filly weren't in the foaling stall.

Mr. Griffen finished picking Renegade's front hoof and turned to Ashleigh. "Dr. Frankel was out an hour ago to check on the filly. He says she looks good, so we turned her and Mary out in the small paddock by themselves. Jonas thinks Slewette should foal tonight." His mouth hardened in a grim line as he looked at Renegade. "We tried breeding another mare with the vet here, but Renegade still wouldn't perform. This colt better make a turnaround soon. The mares are getting ahead of him."

Ashleigh didn't like the discouraging tone of her father's voice. Renegade's race was only a few days away. Maybe if he ran an exceptional race, her parents would be more willing to give him the extra time he needed to settle in and start breeding.

She pulled Stardust to the center of her stall and

began currycombing her fuzzy coat. "You've got to be really good today, Stardust," she warned the mare. "We're ponying Renegade all by ourselves. Promise me?"

Stardust flipped her muzzle up and down and blew noisily through her nostrils.

Ashleigh grinned. "Was that a yes or a no?"

"Here's your saddle, Ash." Mrs. Griffen handed the English saddle and pad over the door. "Nervous?"

Ashleigh slipped the tack into place and nodded.

"Would you feel better if I did the ponying today?" Mrs. Griffen asked, handing Ashleigh the bridle.

Ashleigh glanced up with a stricken look.

"Okay." Her mother smiled. "But we're going to start you out in the big paddock. If everything goes well, next time you can take Renegade out on the track by yourself." She opened Stardust's door and stepped back to let them out. "Remember," she cautioned. "This is a stallion we're working with. I know he's gentle, but don't ever forget you're handling a ton of very valuable and very dangerous horseflesh. If you have any doubts about anything, you stop immediately and ask your father or me for help. Okay?"

Ashleigh nodded. "I'll be careful, Mom."

Ashleigh led Stardust out of the barn and mounted up. She walked the mare into the paddock, then trotted a couple of rounds while she was waiting for her father to bring Renegade in. When the big horse finally stepped out of the barn, Ashleigh's breath caught in her throat. Renegade walked calmly with his head held high, his black mane and tail glistening in the sun. He looked every bit the champion she imagined he could be.

Ashleigh's father helped her clip on the pony rein. She cued Stardust for a walk, and calmly Renegade fell into step beside her. They circled the paddock once before she asked her mare to trot. There was a jolt on her arm when Renegade was slow to follow, but soon the two were trotting around the paddock in tandem.

"This is fun!" Ashleigh said as she passed by her parents. A moment later the bay stallion kicked up his heels and squealed. Stardust took that as a cue to pick up a canter. Ashleigh had her hands full for a lap of the paddock, but she leaned into the reins and brought them both back to a trot.

"That's it, Ash. Keep him at an easy trot for another five minutes, then do four laps at a canter and call it a day," Mr. Griffen instructed. "Rhoda will be here tomorrow to breeze him. He races on Saturday."

Saturday! Ashleigh couldn't help but smile. Renegade would make them proud— she was sure of it.

She finished the workout without a hitch and led Renegade back to the barn. Her parents gave him a bath and walked him cool while she tended to Stardust. She couldn't wait to see Rhoda tomorrow and hear what the girl jockey would have to say after she breezed the stallion for the second time.

The following day at school dragged by for Ashleigh as she watched the clock, waiting for the sound of the last bell so she could hurry home to help with Renegade's work. Rhoda was standing in the driveway with her helmet in hand when Ashleigh ran up the driveway. Stardust and Renegade were already saddled and waiting.

"Hurry up and change your clothes," Mike Smith hollered at her as she came up the driveway. "Rhoda has a race tonight. She's got to get back to the track."

Ashleigh sped up to the house to change her clothes and dashed back out to the barn, where her mother was waiting with Stardust. Ashleigh put her foot in the iron and mounted up, reaching down to run the pony strap through Renegade's bit.

On the way over to the Wortons' she and Rhoda chatted about the upcoming race and the Spiral Stakes, which took place at the end of the month.

"If he runs well on Saturday, I'm going to try to

talk your parents into running him in the Spiral," Rhoda said.

Ashleigh's heart jumped. "Do you really think he's good enough?"

Rhoda shrugged. "He's got go, and if he does well, they'll get a bigger stud fee for him. I don't think it can hurt to try."

Ashleigh smiled all the way to the training track, her mind working. If Renegade won the Kentucky Derby, they wouldn't stop there. They'd enter him in the Preakness and the Belmont—she could be pony- ing the next Triple Crown winner!

They reached the training course and began back- tracking as Mike instructed. Rhoda was to gallop the stallion once around, then breeze him an easy five- eighths of a mile. Ashleigh got them started, then pulled Stardust off the track to wait until the end of their workout.

She sheltered her eyes from the late afternoon sun and watched the big colt move gracefully around the track. When they approached the five-furlong pole the second time around, Rhoda bent low over Renegade's withers and let the reins out a notch. The bay colt took the cue and surged ahead, his powerful muscles rippling as the ground disappeared under his pounding hooves.

Mike started the stopwatch, clocking the furlongs.

"First quarter in twenty-three and change," he said. "That's not exactly what I'd call an easy breeze, but he looks like he's doing it easily."

"Forty-seven seconds for the half," Mike continued. "That's too quick, but he's still going easy." He clicked the stopwatch as the pair crossed the finish line and held it up for Mr. Griffen to see. "Just under a minute for the five furlongs," Mike said with a low whistle. "That's pretty darn good on a slow track and with no pushing from the rider. This colt might turn out to be a better racer than we bargained for."

Rhoda gave Ashleigh a thumbs-up as she pulled Renegade to a halt. "I think you've got a real runner here," she shouted to Mr. and Mrs. Griffen on the rail.

Ashleigh grabbed Renegade as he pulled alongside Stardust. His sides were heaving from the workout, but he'd hardly broken a sweat. She patted the big colt's neck. "Keep up the good work, boy," she said. "You've got a race to win this weekend."

Rhoda dismounted to talk to Mike and her parents, and Ashleigh brought the horses back to Edgardale. She could hear her parents talking excitedly behind them and breathed a big sigh of relief. Today's workout had given them hope. There would be no more talk of selling the stallion now, especially not if he turned out to be a Derby contender.

They reached the barn, and she handed Renegade off to Jonas for a bath. Before Jonas and Rhoda, the trainer made plans for Saturday's race. "Friday he gets a light work to loosen him up. I want Rhoda in the saddle and Ashleigh to go with them to keep this colt slow." Mike smiled. "This big guy seems to like speed, but I want him to save it for the race."

Ashleigh called Mona as soon as Mike and Rhoda were gone and invited her for a quick ride. She couldn't wait to tell her friend all about Renegade. Hurriedly she started her barn chores so they would be done before Mona and Frisky arrived. She was just finishing the last stall when she heard the sound of hoofbeats trotting up the driveway.

"I'm leaving now," Ashleigh called to her parents as she unsnapped Stardust from the crossties where she had been resting.

Mrs. Griffen poked her head out of the feed room. "Dinner will be ready in an hour, Ash. Don't go too far. We're having pizza, and I'm sure Rory would be happy to eat your share if you're late," she joked.

Ashleigh mounted up and waved Mona over to the trails behind the barn.

"Did you ask your mom if you could go with us on Saturday to watch Renegade race?" Ashleigh asked her friend as they started up the trail.

"Yes, of course I'm coming," Mona said. "Can I pose with you guys in the winner's circle?"

"Definitely," Ashleigh promised. "Hey, I'll race you to the big oak tree!" she cried. "Ready? Set? Go!"

Ashleigh leaned low over Stardust's withers the way she'd seen Rhoda time and again. She laughed with glee as she felt the wind in her hair and the stinging slap of her mare's copper mane against her cheeks. She glanced at her friend and saw the same look of excitement on Mona's flushed face.

Frisky pulled ahead by a nose, and Ashleigh asked her mare for more speed. They were almost to the oak tree when Stardust stumbled, tossing her head in the air and slowing her pace. Ashleigh sat back in the saddle to help the mare balance and kept a steadying grip on the reins, bringing Stardust slowly down to a walk and then a halt.

Mona saw the trouble and pulled Frisky up. "What's wrong, Ash?"

"I don't know." Ashleigh jumped from the saddle as soon as Stardust stopped. She groaned when the little chestnut held her right front leg off the ground in pain.

"Did she pull a tendon?" Mona dismounted and took hold of Stardust's head so Ashleigh could examine the mare more closely.

Ashleigh picked up the hoof. "Look, there's a huge stone caught in her hoof!" Ashleigh pulled and pushed on the rock, but it was wedged between the mare's frog and her shoe. It wouldn't come loose. Ashleigh put the hoof down for a moment and looked for something to dig out the stone with.

Stardust stood with her leg out to the side, refusing to put any weight on it. She nudged Ashleigh with her nose and stared at her with her soft, brown eyes.

"I know it hurts, girl." Ashleigh rubbed the mare's blaze. "I'm going to get it out for you." She spotted a thick stick on the side of the road and used it to prod at the lodged stone. Finally it came loose. Ashleigh breathed a sigh of relief and set Stardust's foot back on the ground. "There, is that better?" Ashleigh walked the mare a few steps, but Stardust continued to limp, pointing her head in the direction of the hurt foot as she hobbled down the path.

Mona stayed on the ground to walk beside Ashleigh and Stardust. "I guess it's a good thing we're not very far from home," she said. "Do you want me to ride on ahead and tell your parents?"

Ashleigh shook her head. "Better stay here with us so Stardust doesn't get excited and try to run after you. It looks like a pretty bad stone bruise, but we don't have very far to go."

"If it is bad, you won't be able to ride for at least a week," Mona sympathized.

Ashleigh frowned. But she was supposed to pony Renegade for Rhoda tomorrow. She looked at her limping mare and sighed. Not anymore.

"Looks like you're on your own today, Rhoda," Mike said as he legged her up onto Renegade's back. "Ashleigh will keep you company through the field with Moe, but she won't be able to pony you—Moe's too small."

Ashleigh smiled from her low perch on the pony's back. Her feet practically touched the ground. As she followed Rhoda out of the stable yard and down the trail to the Wortons' farm, Moe had to trot to keep up with the stallion's long-strided walk.

When they reached the track, Mike gave Rhoda instructions for the work.

"Just backtrack him to the other side and trot twice around," Mike instructed. "All I want to do is limber him up for tomorrow's race and take a little bit of the edge off him so he doesn't hurt himself in the stall tonight."

Rhoda nodded and continued onto the track.

Renegade tossed his head, trying to pull more rein from the jockey's hands, but Rhoda pulled him in, asking him to walk. When they reached the turnaround point, the big colt turned quickly and broke into a canter. Rhoda sawed on the reins, forcing him back to a slow trot.

Ashleigh stepped closer to the rail. "Renegade really wants to go today," she remarked. "Rhoda looks like she's having a hard time holding him." She watched as the big bay trotted past them with his nostrils flared and his neck bowed so that his chin almost touched his chest. Rhoda leaned all of her weight into the reins, trying to keep him down to a trot.

Ashleigh watched anxiously. So much depended on tomorrow's race. If Renegade ran well, her parents might be content to keep him and race him in stakes races, holding off on his breeding until next year. But if he ran poorly . . . Ashleigh shuddered. She didn't even want to think about that possibility.

"Looks like he's picking up speed," Mrs. Griffen said, standing on her toes to see.

Mike tapped his fingers nervously on the railing. "I sure wish we had Ashleigh and Stardust out there with them. I don't like the way this is starting to look. That colt's got a full head of steam. And I want him to save every ounce of it for the race tomorrow."

Mr. Griffen shaded his eyes. "They've only got another half mile," he said.

Mike rubbed his chin nervously. "Let's hope he doesn't get away from her before then."

Rhoda trotted past them, her face red from the effort of holding the colt in. Everyone breathed a sigh of relief when the jockey pulled Renegade to a walk and turned him to face the inside rail. Just as Rhoda reached down to pat the big bay, a loud crash sounded from the manure loader in the Wortons' barn.

Rhoda's feet came out of the irons as the big colt bolted. He hesitated when she pulled back on the reins, but then the loader grated noisily against the cement and Renegade took the bit in his teeth, stretching out his neck as he took off down the track. Rhoda clung to his mane, her feet wrapped around his sides, helpless.

"Oh, no." Mike groaned. "I just hope she can keep her balance and stay on."

Renegade pinned his ears flat as he raced against an invisible opponent, galloping faster still.

Mr. Griffen pulled the hat from his head and wrung it in his hands. "Should I step out in front of them?" he suggested.

Mike shook his head. "At the speed he's going, you'd probably get run over or at least get Rhoda hurt if the colt made a sudden turn." Mike sighed. "Without her irons, Rhoda doesn't have any leverage to stop him. Ashleigh, why don't you take Moe out on the track and see if Renegade will stop for you?"

Ashleigh felt her heart jump into her throat. It was up to her to try to slow the runaway colt. She turned Moe up the track and turned him sideways, creating a barrier.

Ashleigh held her breath as Rhoda and Renegade pounded toward them. But the big stallion only veered toward the rail and raced past them to start another lap of the track.

The look of despair on Rhoda's face made Ashleigh feel even more helpless. Moe didn't have enough speed to attempt a pickup, and even if she could get along-side the big horse, Ashleigh doubted if she'd have enough height to grab one of Renegade's reins.

"Looks like they're in for another lap," Mrs. Griffen said with a worried frown.

"He seems to be slowing down a little," Mike observed as they watched Renegade cross the finish line. "Just stay right there," Mike called out to Ashleigh. "Let Rhoda do the rest of the work. He should pull up this time."

Ashleigh's heart pounded in her chest as she saw the horse and rider coming up the track toward her.

This time Renegade stayed in the center of the track, and it looked like he was slowing down. Ashleigh turned Moe's head toward them, and the little pony whinnied a greeting. The stallion's ears pricked, and he slowed down to an easy canter.

Rhoda leaned back in the saddle and pulled on her outside rein, directing Renegade to the outer rail. The big colt kept his eyes on Moe and slowed his pace, bumping down to a trot and blowing a gusty snort through his nostrils.

Ashleigh breathed a sigh of relief when she saw the stallion finally slow to a walk.

"Are you all right?" she called out to Rhoda.

Rhoda nodded, gasping for breath. "That was the wildest ride I've taken in a while," she said in a shaky voice. She looked at Ashleigh and winked. "Next time I think I'll use stirrups!"

Ashleigh laughed and turned Moe back to the gate. The smile froze on her face when she saw the serious looks that greeted them.

"Are you okay?" Mr. Griffen asked Rhoda solemnly. When she nodded, he said, "How about the colt?"

Rhoda reached down to pat Renegade's neck. "It was a heck of a ride, but he didn't bobble any." She tightened the reins as Renegade pranced off the track with his head held high. "I think he'd like to do it again." Rhoda laughed.

Mike took Renegade by the reins, stopping the colt while he ran a hand over his legs. He shook his head in exasperation. "His legs seem fine, but I don't know how we can race him tomorrow when he's already worked over a mile today." He ran a hand through his graying hair. "The other horses in the race are looking pretty good. I think we'd be wasting our time."

Mr. Griffen shoved his hands into his pockets. "What do you want to do, Mike?"

Mike squinted into the sun, then looked back at the Griffens. "I think we should scratch him," he said.

7

"We can't scratch him!" Ashleigh blurted out.

Rhoda ran her hand down Renegade's wet neck. "He's hot, but he's not blowing very hard," she observed. "I don't think that run took that much out of him, Mike," she said.

If Rhoda said Renegade could race, Ashleigh believed her.

"Renegade has to race tomorrow," Ashleigh insisted. She felt her face grow hot, and she lowered her eyes to the ground, but her head snapped up when she heard her father's words.

"Ashleigh's right," Mr. Griffen said. "I'd hate to withdraw from our first race. Rhoda seems confident that Renegade is all right. And some horses do need a bit of a work the day before a race to leg them up."

Mike pursed his lips. "That wasn't a short work,"

he argued. "Renegade won't have anything left for tomorrow. And if he gets beat badly, it won't look good on his record."

Just then a crow flew out of the bushes, cawing noisily. Renegade snorted and gave a little buck, but Rhoda tightened the reins and settled him down. "We're not going for another wild ride today, my friend," she said with a chuckle.

"He doesn't seem all that tired," Mike said, watching the stallion. He looked up at Rhoda. "You really think Renegade's got enough left for tomorrow's race?" he asked.

Rhoda smiled as the big bay jigged in place. "I think so."

Mike heaved a sigh. "I'd prefer to wait another week to race him, Derek, but you're his owners, and I know you're eager to see him perform. We can go ahead and run him tomorrow if that's what you want."

Mr. Griffen looked at his wife.

"Rhoda seems confident," she said, squeezing her husband's hand.

"Okay," Mr. Griffen said. "Let's run him."

Ashleigh stood on the Turfway Park rail between Rory and Mona. Renegade was just trotting past them in the post parade, on his way to the starting gate for his first race for Edgardale. Ashleigh smiled proudly as Rhoda rode past in the farm's new blue-and-white racing silks.

Mona pointed her camera and clicked the button. "These are going to be great pictures, Ash."

"Let's hope we can take some in the winner's circle, too," Ashleigh said nervously.

Mona squeezed her elbow. "You will, Ash. Don't worry."

But Ashleigh was worried. Renegade had been quiet all day, standing in his stall in the receiving barn with his head down, swishing his long tail. They hadn't said anything to her, but she knew her parents were worried, too.

Some of the top three-year-olds in the country paraded past, most of them Derby contenders. Lively Notion was once again favored to win this race despite his loss to Fast Cat a week ago. Ashleigh gulped as Fast Cat pranced past them, kicking up his heels and tossing his head. Renegade was going to have his work cut out for him today.

Renegade made the turn and trotted calmly back to the starting gate. He didn't look like a horse that was about to race. Ashleigh clenched her teeth. If Renegade ran poorly today, there would be no hope for entering the stallion in the Spiral Stakes, let alone the Derby. And if he continued to refuse to breed, her parents would be forced to sell him.

Renegade had drawn the number-three post position. He stood patiently, waiting for the other horses to enter the gate.

"He sure looks quiet," Mona commented.

Ashleigh pursed her lips and held her breath until the last horse was loaded in.

"And they're off!" the announcer called over the loud clang of the starting gate doors and the ringing of the bell.

"Royal Renegade comes out on top and is running handily along the inside rail," the announcer called. "Lively Notion is second by a length, with Annie's Choice in third and Fast Cat coming up on the outside as the horses move into the clubhouse turn."

"He's winning!" Mona screamed, jumping up and down.

Ashleigh's eyes never left the bay colt on the lead. This was only the beginning of the race—there was still a long way to go. She glanced quickly at the tote board to see what the first-quarter fraction was: twenty-three seconds flat. It wasn't a record breaker, but it was still pretty fast. After Renegade's last race Mike had thought the colt was a come-from-behind horse, but the bay stallion was doing a great job of running out front. Ashleigh hoped he could maintain the lead.

The horses moved down the back side with Renegade still in front.

"Fast Cat makes his move on the inside," the announcer said. "He moves into third place with Lively Notion holding on for second."

Ashleigh stood on her tiptoes to see the horses as they went into the top turn. "He's still in first place," she said in awe. The tote board showed the half mile being run in forty-six and change. Renegade was setting speed-horse fractions, but could he keep it up?

"They come out of the turn and down the stretch!" the announcer cried. "Annie's Choice fades into the pack as Fast Cat moves up to challenge the leader along with Lively Notion."

"Come on, Renegade!" Ashleigh yelled as loud as she could. "You can do it!"

"Fast Cat is catching him," Mona groaned. "Rhoda better do something quick."

As the other horse moved up to challenge from the outside, Rhoda flipped her whip into position and showed it to Renegade. The big horse needed no further encouragement. He pulled ahead by first one length and then another.

The announcer's voice boomed over the speaker

system. "Royal Renegade is running away from the herd. He's opened up three lengths on them and is pulling away!"

The cameras flashed as Renegade crossed the finish line. Ashleigh jumped up and down, hugging Mona and Rory. "We did it! We won!" she cried.

Mr. and Mrs. Griffen and Caroline met them at the winner's circle. Mike walked out onto the track to wait for Renegade and Rhoda to return. He shook his head in disbelief.

Renegade trotted up with his sides heaving and his nostrils distended to their fullest. Ashleigh could see the soft pink lining of his nose as his chest heaved in and out. The proud stallion tossed his head as he stepped into the winner's circle.

"I can't believe it," Mike said as he held the bay colt's head for the win photo. "This colt has never gone wire to wire before. I figured him for a closer. I just can't believe he held out with those fractions!"

Rhoda leaned down to pat Renegade's foam-flecked neck. "This is one great horse, Mr. and Mrs. Griffen. I'd like to ride him in the Spiral Stakes if you'll let me. I think we could win that one, too!"

Mike grinned. "And from there we might be on to the Derby!"

Ashleigh's heart soared to hear the very words

she'd been imagining in her head spoken out loud by the respected trainer.

"Why doesn't everyone come by the house tomorrow, and we'll discuss our plans for this guy's future?" Mr. Griffen suggested. "Renegade may have problems as a breeder, but we might as well try to recoup some of our money racing him."

Ashleigh was smiling so widely, she was sure all the win photo would capture of her was a face full of teeth. The camera flashed, and she blinked hard, feeling like she was in a dream world. When her vision cleared, she hugged Renegade around the neck. "I knew you could do it, boy," she told him. "And this is just the beginning!"

Ashleigh was surprised at how many people at her school had heard of Renegade's success by Monday morning. She smiled shyly as people she didn't even know congratulated her.

"That is too cool," Ashleigh's friends Jamie Wilson and Lynne Duran cried as they sat down next to her and Mona in the lunchroom. Lynne's father was an announcer at Churchill Downs, so she was always up on all the latest racing news.

"My father says he thinks Renegade might have a

shot at the Kentucky Derby if he keeps winning like he did today," Lynne said.

Jamie pulled a ham sandwich from her bag and took a huge bite, nodding in agreement.

Ashleigh finished out the school day in a sort of daydream. It was difficult to concentrate when all she could see was a blanket of roses being placed over Renegade's withers at the Kentucky Derby.

On the bus ride home Ashleigh and Mona made plans to play with Mary and Slewette's new foals the next day after school. Stardust's foot was better, but Ashleigh wanted to wait another day before even thinking about riding her. She brought an apple to her mare and talked to her for a bit before continuing on to bring Renegade a treat.

Mr. Griffen was checking the stallion over when Ashleigh arrived at his stall. He looked worried. "Is something the matter?" Ashleigh asked.

Mr. Griffen ran a hand through his dark hair. "We tried covering Slewette again today and no go. We may need to sell Renegade if he refuses to breed."

Ashleigh gasped. "But if he's running well and earning purse money, why would we sell him?"

Mr. Griffen shook his head. "Edgardale is a *breeding* farm, Ashleigh. Don't forget that." He stroked the bay stallion's muzzle. "It's great that Renegade might win some money for us. But racing is too risky. We need a good stallion who will cover all our mares and bring in stud fees."

Ashleigh felt like she had just been punched in the stomach. She had thought that winning his last race would bide time for Renegade, but it just made him easier to sell.

Mr. Griffen turned to go, but he paused. "How's your mare's stone bruise coming?" he asked.

"She's not limping now," Ashleigh said. "That poultice Jonas gave me really worked."

Mr. Griffen scratched his chin. "How would you feel about ponying Renegade for a slow walk around the front paddock tomorrow?"

Ashleigh nodded, trying to work up some enthusiasm, but she couldn't get over the depressing fact that her parents would still want to sell Renegade even though he was racing well.

"He's not ready to go back to work yet," Mr. Griffen said. "But Mike thinks it would help limber Renegade up if we walked him out."

"Sure," Ashleigh said weakly.

Later that night Ashleigh sat on her bed, studying the latest issues of the *Daily Racing Form* and trying not to think about losing Renegade. A photo on the front page of a small Virginia paper caught her atten-

tion. The horse in the picture bore a striking resemblance to Renegade. She checked the date on the
Racing Form. It was only a week old.

She read the caption, surprised when she saw the
horse's name. "Royal Rebel," Ashleigh whispered. She
quickly scanned the article. The horse might have a
similar name to Renegade and almost identical looks,
but he certainly didn't have the same speed. Royal
Rebel had been expected to win his first race, but after
leading the field for five furlongs he had faded back to
last place, losing the race by thirty lengths.

"Come on, Ash, lights out," Caroline insisted,
pulling the covers over her head grumpily.

Ashleigh tossed the *Racing Form*s on the nightstand
and rolled over to turn off the light. She breathed
deeply, trying not to let her worries keep her awake.

Ashleigh stared out the windows of the school bus at
the newly green fields. Spring was coming. The trees
were beginning to bud, and early flowers were pushing
up through the dirt. Most of the mares had foaled, and
the Kentucky pastures were full of frolicking colts and
fillies and their mothers.

Ashleigh sighed. Edgardale wouldn't have any foals

at all next year if Renegade didn't change his tune about breeding.

The school bus braked to a halt at their stop, and Ashleigh waved to Mona as they went their separate ways. It had been a week since Ashleigh had last ridden her mare. Stardust wasn't ready for any fast work yet, but a nice walk around the farm would do her good.

Mrs. Griffen had Stardust saddled by the time Ashleigh changed her clothes and made her way out to the barn.

"Here's your helmet, kiddo," Mrs. Griffen said as she held Stardust for Ashleigh to mount. "Your dad's bringing Renegade out. He'll meet you at the front paddock."

Ashleigh asked Stardust for a walk, paying close attention to how she was stepping. The mare didn't seem to have any soreness in her injured foot. Ashleigh was tempted to trot, but she knew it would be better to wait a few more days before she tried anything faster than a walk.

A loud whinny split the air. Ashleigh and Stardust turned to see Renegade entering the paddock. Stardust trumpeted a welcome call to the big stallion. "Don't be such a flirt," Ashleigh scolded.

Ashleigh reached down to take the lead rope from her father.

"Just walk him around in here for about ten minutes, Ash. I'll be back to get him." Mr. Griffen returned to the barn to finish his chores.

Ashleigh pulled Renegade in close to Stardust's shoulder. They walked in companionable silence for a few rounds, then Renegade brushed his lips in Stardust's mane and nickered to her. Stardust bumped against the bay stallion and nickered back.

"Don't be setting up a date with my girl," Ashleigh teased as she reached over to tousle Renegade's black mane.

Renegade nibbled at Stardust's crest, and the mare arched her neck and squealed. She was answered by a couple of interested snorts from the stallion.

"Uh-oh, it looks like you're coming into season," Ashleigh said to the mare. "We may not be able to pony Renegade for a few days."

Ashleigh's head popped up as she thought about what she had just said. Renegade was showing signs of interest in Stardust. She knew the stallion was comfortable with the copper-colored mare. If Renegade would breed with Stardust, maybe he would be less shy about the other mares.

It was a long shot, but Ashleigh was desperate to try anything to convince her parents to keep Renegade. After Dr. Frankel's comment about Secretariat being a shy breeder, Ashleigh had read up on the famous race-horse in her parents' horse books. Secretariat had finally been won over to breeding and had finished his life on a stud farm. The same thing could happen to Renegade.

An idea began to form in her mind. It was risky, but Renegade's future and the future of Edgardale were both at stake. Ashleigh finished up her chores for the night and waited until everyone had gone up to the house for dinner. Then she picked up the barn tele-phone and called Mona to tell her friend her plan.

8

"Ashleigh, you can't!" Mona cried. "Your parents will ground you for life!"

Ashleigh shifted the phone to her other ear. "But I'll make it look like an accident. Once Stardust is bred, my parents will see that there is hope for Renegade as a stud," Ashleigh argued. "Plus Stardust will have Renegade's foal!"

"But what if it doesn't work, Ash?" Mona said doubtfully. "What if Stardust or Renegade gets hurt?"

"I have to try," Ashleigh said. She froze when she heard a noise coming from Jonas's apartment.

"But how?" Mona asked. "My parents would ground me forever if anything went wrong."

Ashleigh lowered her voice, keeping her eye on the barn door in case one of her parents returned. "I always like to check on the horses before I go to bed. I've got

Stardust in the paddock next to Renegade right now. All I have to do is open the gate between them."

Ashleigh closed her eyes and rubbed her forehead. "I'm sure I'll get in a lot of trouble for being careless enough to leave the gate unlatched, but if things work out, my parents won't mind so much."

"Yeah." Mona chuckled. "They'll only ground you until you're eighteen and feed you nothing but bread and water. You'll definitely be skinny enough to be a jockey," Mona teased.

Ashleigh tried to laugh, but her stomach was tied in knots at the thought of what she was about to do. She said good-bye to Mona, placed the phone back on its hook, and headed into the house for dinner before her parents came looking for her. As she passed by the paddocks, Stardust's shrill squeal pierced the air, followed by answering snorts from Renegade. Hearing them gave Ashleigh a shred of hope. They were certainly getting along well.

Her mother had made lasagna, one of her favorite dishes. Ashleigh dished up a big helping of the pasta, her eyes catching sight of a horse magazine lying on the kitchen counter. The cover showed a picture of the track at Churchill Downs. Ashleigh ate slowly, imagining Renegade in the winner's circle at the famous track on Derby Day. But he'd be running for another farm unless she did something to keep him at Edgardale.

Just as Ashleigh finished her dinner and was about to ask to be excused, a mare's screaming whinnies and Renegade's furious trumpeting could be heard from the barnyard.

"What in the world?" Mr. Griffen said, bolting from his chair.

Mrs. Griffen and Ashleigh were right behind him.

"But there's no mare near Renegade," Mrs. Griffen said in confusion. "What's he making all the fuss about?"

As they raced for the door, Ashleigh tried to hide her guilty look. "I put Stardust in the paddock next to Renegade," she admitted. "They get along really well, and I thought Renegade could use the company."

They ran out the door and down the steps to the barn, stopping when they came into view of Stardust and the stallion, standing nose to nose in Stardust's paddock. Renegade had broken through the gate on his own.

Jonas rushed out to join them. "I tried to call him off before she was bred," Jonas said between huffs. "I think we're too late."

Ashleigh tried to hide her smile. Even though she had fully intended to turn the two horses out together, they had managed to do it on their own. But she knew she'd still be in trouble.

Mrs. Griffen turned to Ashleigh, eyeing her suspiciously. She heaved an exasperated breath. "Well, what's done is done. Let's get Stardust out of there."

Mr. Griffen frowned and grabbed the mare's halter. "I'm glad to see that there's hope for Renegade, but I'm very disappointed that Stardust was the mare he decided to cover."

Jonas smiled. "At least we know he will breed when he wants to. We can call the vet in the morning and see if we can get some of our other mares bred."

Mr. Griffen nodded. "You're right, Jonas. I'm just a little upset that Renegade's first foal is going to be of no use to us," he said, looking at Stardust disapprovingly.

Ashleigh crossed her arms, upset to hear her father talk about Stardust like she was a mutt. Stardust was beautiful, even if she wasn't pure Thoroughbred! A foal out of her and Renegade would be great no matter what! She hugged herself at the thought. Stardust might be carrying a Thoroughbred foal!

"I want to talk to you later, young lady," Mr. Griffen told Ashleigh.

Ashleigh felt a knot in the pit of her stomach. She hadn't heard her father this angry since the time she had raced Moe against Frisky and the pony had gotten injured.

Elaine Griffen gave Ashleigh a nudge toward the house.

"Ashleigh had no way of knowing that Renegade would break down the gate to get in with Stardust, Derek," she pleaded in Ashleigh's defense. "And the horses are fine. Let's just call it a night."

Mr. Griffen nodded, dismissing Ashleigh with a tilt of his head.

Ashleigh knew better than to hang around. In actual fact, she was in much less trouble than she could have been. She ran up the steps of the house and headed straight for the phone to call Mona and tell her the good news.

"I can't believe Stardust is going to have a Thoroughbred baby!" Mona said excitedly as they stepped off the school bus the following day.

Ashleigh hugged her schoolbooks to her and smiled. "Well, we won't know if she's in foal until we have her checked in another thirty days," she said.

Mona waved good-bye to their friends on the bus as it pulled away. "Maybe someday your parents will let me breed Frisky to Renegade, and we could have colts that were related."

"Yeah," Ashleigh agreed. "Frisky is registered with The Jockey Club. Your foal would be papered, and you could even race it!"

Mona's face lit up at the thought. The girls slapped each other a high five and slung their backpacks over their shoulders, heading for home.

"Who's that?" Mona asked, pointing down the way at a truck and horse trailer that were pulled over to the side of the road. "It kind of looks like the horse trailer Renegade was delivered in."

Ashleigh squinted to look into the sun. "Yeah, but it's a different truck. I hope it's not Mr. Rolland—he gives me the creeps."

"We should probably see if they need help," Mona said. "It looks like there's a horse in the trailer."

As they got closer to the vehicle, Ashleigh could see a man fixing a flat tire. She felt a jolt of recognition when she saw the beat-up old trailer and realized that Mona was right—the trailer *did* look like the one Renegade had been delivered in, but she didn't recognize the truck or the large, rough-looking man who knelt in the gravel on the side of the road.

"*Is* this the trailer Renegade was delivered in?" Mona asked as she ran her eyes over the scratched and dented vehicle.

"I'm not sure," Ashleigh said in confusion. "Didn't

Mr. Rolland's trailer have a silver stripe on it?"

Mona shrugged. "I can't remember. It was so beat up, I didn't pay much attention to it."

The man was just finishing the repair job as they approached. He rose to his feet, towering over the girls as he tossed the flat tire into the bed of the pickup like it weighed nothing. "What do you want?" he asked gruffly, staring at them with beady blue eyes.

Ashleigh backed up a step and gulped. "W-we were just checking to see if you needed any help," she managed to squeak out. "We saw you had a horse in the trailer, and we thought you might need us to call somebody for you."

Just then the horse in question pushed his nose against the little door in the front of the rusty old trailer and popped it open. Ashleigh's mouth dropped open, and her heart skipped a beat when she saw the large bay head with the white blaze and black forelock. Mona poked her hard in the ribs.

"No need to go calling anybody," the large man said. "I got the tire fixed all by myself. I'll just go on about my business now, and you girls go back to your own."

"Wh-whose horse is that?" Mona stammered.

The big man cocked his head and squinted at them through one eye. "Nosy little things, aren't you?" he drawled as he reached up to slam the trailer door shut. "This here is *my* horse, and I'm taking him home." He waved his hand. "Now, you two shoo before I get upset," he warned.

He got into his truck and started the engine, watching them coldly in the rearview mirror.

Mona grabbed Ashleigh by the arm, and they turned and ran a few hundred feet before stopping to look back at the departing vehicle.

Ashleigh threw her book bag on the ground as she gasped for air. Her heart was pounding in her throat. "Mona, that horse was Renegade. I think that man just stole him!" she gasped. "We've got to go get help!"

9

Ashleigh ran up the driveway toward Edgardale with Mona close on her heels. She could feel the air burning in and out of her lungs as she pumped her arms and legs, trying to go faster. By now the man had probably reached the highway or taken any number of back roads to make his getaway.

Ashleigh flew up the stairs to her house, taking the steps two at a time. "Mom, Dad!" she hollered as she jerked open the front door. She ran from room to room, but the house was empty. "They must be down at the barn," Ashleigh said, and raced back outside.

"Jonas!" Ashleigh cried as she spotted the old groom unloading grain from the pickup into the feed shed. She stopped beside him, her legs trembling. "Where are my parents? I think someone stole Renegade!" she told him, gulping for air.

Mona ran to Ashleigh's side. "We've got to hurry," she said urgently. "He's going to get away!"

Jonas looked back and forth between them. "What are you talking about?" he asked. "Renegade's in his paddock. I just got back from the feed store about five minutes ago. He was screaming for his oats before I even stepped from the truck. Your parents and Rory are up in the north pasture, worming the yearlings."

Ashleigh heard a loud whinny from Renegade's paddock. She walked to his stall and peeked over the door. The big bay stallion was right where Jonas said he would be—running up and down the fence line, calling for his dinner.

"What made you think Renegade was stolen?" Jonas asked.

Ashleigh shrugged, feeling the color rise to her cheeks. It had been very silly of her to jump to that conclusion. There were a lot of bay horses with blazes. And she hadn't gotten a very good look at the horse before the man had slammed the door. "It was nothing," she told the old stable hand. "I made a mistake."

"Nothing?" Jonas looked at her skeptically. "Don't be playing about stuff like that, Ashleigh," he warned.

"I don't get it," Mona said in disbelief after Jonas turned away and went back to his chores. "I was so sure that was Renegade in the horse trailer."

Ashleigh pursed her lips, watching as the big colt pranced up and down the fence, flipping his head and kicking out at the boards. "I was fooled, too," Ashleigh admitted. "I didn't get to see if the horse in that trailer had a white front sock, but his head sure looked a lot like Renegade's."

Mona still looked puzzled. "He even sounded like Renegade when he whinnied."

Ashleigh leaned on the door and breathed a huge sigh of relief. "I feel kind of silly now."

Mona nodded in agreement. "At least we found out before we chased him down the road in a car."

Ashleigh opened the stall door. "Wait here," she said to Mona. "Renegade looks kind of upset. I'm going out to see what's the matter with him."

She closed the door behind her and walked out into the paddock. Renegade stopped pacing and turned to fix his gaze on her. He lifted his head and snorted. "It's okay," Ashleigh said. She extended her hand and walked toward the bay stallion. When she was within six feet of him, Renegade whirled and showed her his heels, kicking up a spray of dirt in her face.

Ashleigh was shocked. Renegade had never done anything like that before. He knew better.

"Ashleigh, why don't you come out of there?" Mona said in concern. "Renegade seems kind of crazy today."

Jonas entered Renegade's stall, hanging a hay net from the hook on the wall. "The colt acts like a whole new horse now that he's breeding," he said. "Dr. Frankel was by this morning, and we got Renegade to breed two out of the four mares. It looks like we might be keeping this stallion and going to the Kentucky Derby after all!"

Renegade saw his dinner being served and trotted toward his stall.

"Better get on out of here before he comes in to eat," Jonas warned.

Ashleigh hurried out of the stall, and the stallion came charging in to eat his hay. Renegade took two big mouthfuls of grass hay, then turned and pinned his ears fiercely at the girls.

Mona stepped back, dragging Ashleigh with her. "Wow, he sure has changed!" she said in surprise. "All of this is from breeding a couple of mares?"

Ashleigh pulled a piece of straw from a nearby bale, fumbling with it before breaking it into many pieces. "Some stallions get mean when they start breeding, but Renegade was always so sweet," she said. "I didn't think he'd change this much."

Ashleigh stuffed her hands into her pockets. "Guess I better head back to the house and change for my chores." She walked Mona to the gate and said good-bye. Stardust was out in the front paddock, munching on a few new shoots of grass that were poking through the ground. Ashleigh watched her for a moment. It had been her idea to breed Stardust to Renegade. She hoped the stallion's disposition hadn't changed so much, it affected his racing.

That night at the dinner table Ashleigh chose to keep quiet about seeing the horse trailer with the horse that looked like Renegade. She hoped Jonas wouldn't mention it to her parents, either. She still felt foolish making such wild accusations. She also felt a little hurt that Renegade had kicked out at her. She had thought they were friends. Ashleigh nibbled at her salad. Her parents were right—stallions were very unpredictable!

"Well," Mr. Griffen said, lifting his water glass as if to make a toast. "Here's to Renegade. It looks like we're going to be able to keep him at stud, and Mike wants to enter him in the Spiral Stakes. Rhoda will be out to work him tomorrow."

Ashleigh clinked glasses with her father, thrilled that things were finally looking up for the big bay stallion. But in the back of her mind was a lingering dread she couldn't dispel, despite her parents' smiles.

• • •

"Rhoda will be here soon," Mrs. Griffen announced. She handed Ashleigh a stack of *Daily Racing Form*s. "These should keep you busy until she gets here. The total rundown for Renegade's last race is in the back of the top one."

Ashleigh flipped through the top issue. She smiled when she saw that Renegade had actually beaten the two Derby favorites by three-and-a-half lengths. She scanned the rest of the columns, looking to see if any of Edgardale's colts were listed. She saw the name Royal Rebel, and she read the results of the colt's last race.

Ashleigh tucked a lock of hair behind her ear and shook her head in sympathy. Rebel's second race was exactly like his first. He'd started out the cheap claiming race out front and then given up about five furlongs into the mile. She whistled when she saw the fractions the colt had set. With a forty-six-second half mile, she wondered why Rebel's trainer wasn't running him in sprint races, where he had more of a shot at winning.

Ashleigh looked at Rebel's information, noting that he was a four-year-old. She knew that if the colt didn't win a race at a recognized track by the time he was five, The Jockey Club wouldn't allow him to race anymore.

Ashleigh's breath caught in her throat when she read the name of the listed owner—Dave Rolland. She wondered if he was any relation to the creepy trainer they had purchased Renegade from. Ashleigh's thoughts were interrupted by the sound of the barn door rolling open.

"Let's go," Mike said, walking into the barn with Rhoda on his heels. "I hear Renegade has been living up to his name lately. I want to work him a half mile today and see if we can take a little of that edge off. I don't want him blowing a big race like the Spiral because he's too wound up."

Ashleigh put away the *Racing Forms* and led Stardust out of the barn. She mounted up, then waited for Rhoda to mount Renegade. She leaned forward to put the ponying rope through Renegade's bit as Rhoda walked up beside them, but Renegade pulled his head away and lunged at her arm, his teeth bared. Ashleigh jerked her arm back in shock. Rhoda hauled on Renegade's bit, giving him a boot in the side for misbehaving.

"Are you all right, Ash?" Rhoda asked. "That was a surprise. Renegade's never tried biting you before, has he?"

Ashleigh rubbed her arm, glaring accusingly at the big bay. "Renegade has been acting kind of funny the last couple of days," she said. She reached down again to attach the pony rope, but this time she kept her eye on the unpredictable colt.

Renegade pranced all the way to the training track. Ashleigh felt like her arm was ready to fall off by the time they stepped onto the Wortons' oval track.

"I bet we turn in a great time today," Rhoda said, winding the reins around her fists. "You only have to back us up a little ways, Ash. I'm going to gallop him around once to get the kinks out before and then let him out the last half mile."

"Good luck," Ashleigh said, turning them loose. She waited until the bay was a ways down the track before she turned Stardust and trotted after him, stopping when she reached the pickup point.

Rhoda began the work, and Ashleigh followed Renegade's progress around the track. The stallion tossed his head and fought Rhoda's hands. His stride looked short and choppy. She hoped he wasn't getting lame.

On the second trip around the track Rhoda asked Renegade to move out a few strides before the half-mile pole. Ashleigh saw the colt pin his ears as he picked up speed, sprinting around the turn to the finish line.

Mike clicked the stopwatch. "Forty-six and change!"

he shouted. "I think this colt's going to give them a run for their money in the Spiral."

They rode the horses back to Edgardale, and Rhoda drove off in her little red car.

"Need some help with Renegade's bath?" Ashleigh volunteered.

Mr. Griffen shook his head. "I think Jonas and I will handle Renegade's cooling out today," he said. "He's been quite a handful. In fact, I think it might be a good idea to hold off on breeding him until after the Spiral."

Jonas was scraping the water off the stallion's belly. He jumped back as Renegade cow kicked to the side. "I think you're right," he said in astonishment. "Breeding has made him ornery."

Later that night Ashleigh volunteered to do the final barn check with Jonas before everyone retired for bed.

Ashleigh grabbed a handful of carrots from the tack room, giving one to Stardust before moving on to Renegade's stall. The stallion pressed up against the front of the stall, banging on the wood with his hoof, begging for the treat.

Ashleigh broke the carrot in two, offering her palm

to the stallion's outstretched lips. Renegade snapped up the treat and chewed greedily. Ashleigh broke off another piece for him, but when she couldn't get the treat to the stallion fast enough, the big bay reached out and nipped her on the shoulder.

"Ouch!" Ashleigh cried. "What did you do that for?" She looked at the stallion accusingly. "I thought we were friends." The nip had hurt her arm, but not as much as it had hurt her feelings. What was happening to Renegade? Why didn't he like her anymore?

Jonas poked his head out of the foaling stall. "Is everything all right?" he called.

Ashleigh turned and nodded to Jonas, but when she looked back at Renegade, she couldn't help but frown. Everything *wasn't* all right.

Ashleigh wove her way through the fans at Turfway Park. The Spiral Stakes race was popular, so the crowd was big. Everyone wanted to get a glimpse of the Derby contenders and make their own guess as to who would go all the way. Ashleigh squeezed in on the rail beside Mike and stood on her toes to get the best view.

The horses were just leaving the walking ring, parading in front of the tote board so the racing fans could get a good look at the horses they were betting on. The sun was shining brightly, flowers were starting to bloom on the infield, and the trees were green. It was a perfect day for a race!

"What do you think, Mike?" Ashleigh asked, noting the frown on the trainer's face.

Mike ran a hand nervously over his face. "Look at him," he said, pointing to where Rhoda and Renegade were parading in front of the crowd. "He's all lathered up. He never heats up like that before a race. Something's not right. Maybe I should have scratched him."

Ashleigh looked closely at the stallion as he passed by at a trot. Renegade was covered in lather from head to hoof. Mike was right. Something was very wrong.

"He looks like he's already run his race," Mike said. "But by the odds on the tote board, the crowd likes him. They've got him picked to run second."

The announcer's voice broke over the noise of the crowd, calling the horses to the post. "They're heading for the gate for this year's running of the mile-and-an-eighth Spiral Stakes!"

Ashleigh leaned on the railing, watching as the horses were led into the gate. Renegade balked, refusing to enter the gate, and reared with Rhoda when the gate man grabbed one of his reins. Finally the big bay gave in, and they closed the bar behind him.

Butterflies fluttered in Ashleigh's stomach. Something was wrong with Renegade, and it had all started when she tried to breed Stardust.

"They're in," the announcer called. "And they're off for the running of the Spiral Stakes! Royal Renegade breaks on top and goes straight to the front, followed by Fast Cat and Gotcha Covered on the inside. High

Melody is in fourth, and it's several lengths back to the rest of the field."

"Look at him go!" Ashleigh cried as Renegade flew into the clubhouse turn, opening up several lengths on the rest of the field. Her brows drew together, and she turned to Mike in confusion. "I thought you told Rhoda to hold him to the middle of the pack to save his energy, then make a run down the homestretch. Why is he out front?"

Renegade continued to open up the lead, and Mike glanced up at the tote board to check the first quarter-mile fraction. "Twenty-two and change for the quarter mile. That's not right." He shook his head. "Renegade has speed, but he's never run those kind of fractions in a race. He can't last at that pace. Especially not over the distance of a mile and an eighth."

Ashleigh lost the horses as they came out of the turn and disappeared behind the large tote board. When they exited on the other side, Renegade was even farther out front.

"What in the world is Rhoda thinking?" Mike cried angrily.

Even from as far away as they were, Ashleigh could see that Rhoda was pulling tightly on Renegade's reins, trying to get him under control.

The announcer's voice boomed over the sound

system. "Royal Renegade still holds the lead by six lengths as they come out of the turn and down the backstretch! Fast Cat is in second, and Gotcha Covered drops out of contention. High Melody is making a bold move on the outside."

"Come on, Renegade!" Ashleigh shouted. But as the horses raced past the half-mile pole, posting a speed of forty-five seconds for the half, Ashleigh could see Renegade begin to falter.

"Fast Cat is closing ground on the leader, with High Melody moving alongside," the announcer called.

Ashleigh gasped as Renegade passed the five-eighths marker and then seemed to freeze in his tracks. Fast Cat raced by him with the rest of the field right behind him. "No!" she cried as she stood on her toes to keep track of Rhoda's blue-and-white silks. The colors faded farther and farther back until they stood out clearly in last place.

Ashleigh felt a tear slip down her cheek as Fast Cat and High Melody raced across the finish line. It took a few more seconds for the rest of the field to complete the race, followed by Renegade, looking totally worn out, as he cantered across the wire with faltering steps.

The rest of the Griffen family pushed through the crowd, coming to stand beside Mike and Ashleigh. Mr. Griffen placed a hand on Mike's shoulder. "Do you think Renegade's all right? Maybe he pulled something going into the gate."

"He seemed to be traveling fine," Mike said. "It looked like he just got tired."

Mike's shoulders slumped as they stepped onto the track to wait for Renegade. When Rhoda and Renegade trotted up, Ashleigh was amazed at how exhausted the horse looked. His coat was covered in dirt from running at the back of the herd, and his coat was soaked through. The stallion's muscles quivered as Rhoda hopped off and pulled her racing saddle from his back.

"I'm not sure what happened out there, but this is a different horse than the one I raced two weeks ago," she said. She brushed a stray tendril of hair from her hot, sticky face. "He came out of the gate like a rocket. I couldn't keep him rated," Rhoda said. "He just took the bit and ran like a crazy horse, then he totally gave out on me before we reached three-quarters of a mile." She shook her head at Mr. and Mrs. Griffen. "I don't know what to tell you folks. I tried my best. He just didn't have it today."

Mr. Griffen nodded. "We'll take the colt home to rest and see if we can figure out what went wrong," he said. "I know you did your best, Rhoda. We'll see you at the farm next week."

They followed Mike and Renegade back to the

barn. A track official was waiting for them when they got there.

"Sorry, Mike," the official apologized. "But you've been called to the test barn. Bring the colt in right now. Someone can fetch your buckets and blankets and bring them to you."

Mike pulled out his set of keys and handed them to Mr. Griffen. "Derek, could you and Elaine run back to my tack room and get Renegade's things?"

"Why do we have to go to the test barn?" Ashleigh asked, surprised. "I thought they only tested the winner." She frowned at Renegade, who was plodding along with his head down, his sides still heaving in exertion.

Mike turned to Ashleigh. "This happens sometimes when a horse doesn't run as well as expected. They want to make sure no one has tampered with the horse, maybe given him drugs to make him run poorly. They'll give Renegade a urine test, just like they do for the winners."

Ashleigh's head snapped up. "Do you think somebody could have drugged Renegade?"

Mike shook his head. "Any drugs in this horse's system will go against me," he explained. "The horse is my responsibility. Unless I have valid proof that somebody else drugged him, I could lose my license. As the owners, your parents could be in trouble, too."

Ashleigh gasped. She knew Mike didn't drug his horses, but somebody could have gotten to Renegade. Why else would the horse run so differently from his usual style?

Caroline and Rory ran to catch up to Ashleigh and Mike while their parents gathered Renegade's things. "Do you really think someone gave our horse drugs?" Caroline asked when she caught the tail end of the conversation.

Mike circled Renegade outside the test barn, waiting to be let in. "Renegade was pretty closely watched before the race. I don't think anyone could have gotten to him. But it is a possibility. I really thought we had a chance to win that race. The colt just didn't run like himself."

Mr. and Mrs. Griffen arrived with the wash buckets and cool-out blanket just as Mike led Renegade into the test barn with Ashleigh right behind them.

"Sorry, folks," Ashleigh heard the guard say. "Only the trainer and one helper allowed inside per horse."

Mike and Ashleigh washed the tired stallion and hooked him on the hot walker in the testing area. They stood next to the fence while Renegade was cooling out so they could talk to the others.

"What are we going to do with him now?" Mrs.

Griffen asked. "Is anyone going to want to breed their mares to him after a performance like that?"

Mike studied the stallion as he slowly circled the ring. "For now all we can do is take him home and see how he comes out of this." Mike shut off the hot walker and nodded for Ashleigh to give Renegade a drink. "Not too much at a time," Mike warned. "We don't need him colicking on us." He turned the hot walker back on and watched as the big horse circled around with his head hanging low. "Maybe he's coming down with something. Let's wait a few days and see what happens."

Ashleigh studied Renegade. She couldn't believe the difference between this race and the last one he had won. Everyone had been so sure that the colt could win the Spiral Stakes—her especially! Ashleigh plopped down on a bale of straw and sighed. Only a week ago she had been dreaming of entering Renegade in the Derby. Now those dreams were fading fast. Where had they gone wrong?

Fifteen minutes later, when Renegade was all cooled off and the test was complete, they walked him back to the barn and prepared to load him into the trailer for the ride home. Mike handed Ashleigh a couple of the *Daily Racing Form*s from the betting booths at the front side of the track. "Here," he said. "Your mom said you might like these. There are some different papers from other states, too. They're from today's races."

"Thanks," Ashleigh said gratefully.

"I'll see you guys tomorrow," Mike said. "I've got a horse going at Churchill Downs tomorrow."

Ashleigh perked up. "Can I go?" She loved to visit the beautiful old track with its twin white steeples and lovely grounds.

"Ashleigh!" Mrs. Griffen reprimanded. "You know it's not polite to invite yourself to places. Mike's busy. He doesn't have time to keep his eye on you."

Mike chuckled. "I'd love to have the company. Ashleigh is always welcome to ride along." He winked at Ashleigh. "I'll be there bright and early. Are you sure that's how you want to spend your Sunday morning?"

Ashleigh nodded vigorously. It would give her something to look forward to after this disastrous week with Renegade.

True to his word, Mike pulled into Edgardale at seven o'clock the following morning.

"Any word on Renegade's test?" Mr. Griffen asked.

Mike shook his head. "We won't know until ten

o'clock today. How's the big guy look this morning?"

"Tired," Mr. Griffen said. "With the fractions he set for the quarter and the half mile, I'm not a bit surprised. Dr. Frankel is coming out this morning to check him."

Ashleigh tuned out the conversation as the two men began idly chatting about the weather and feed prices. She sat down on a bale of straw with the *Daily Racing Form*s that Mike had given her the night before and flipped through the pages, looking for anything of interest.

She found Renegade's statistics. She looked over his record, comparing yesterday's race to his previous races. It didn't make any sense. His times for the first half of the Spiral Stakes were way faster than the fractions he had set in his other races. Had breeding those mares changed him that much?

Ashleigh put down the paper and sighed. They had to be missing something. Something had to be wrong for a horse to make that big of a change. She couldn't wait to hear the results of last night's test and see what Dr. Frankel would say after examining Renegade later in the morning.

She flipped through the rest of the *Racing Form*s, spying the one from Virginia. That was where Royal Rebel was from. Ashleigh's curiosity in Royal Rebel was growing. He bore such a striking resemblance to Renegade and had a similar name, but the fact that Dave Rolland was listed as his owner really piqued Ashleigh's interest.

"Let's go, Ash," Mike hollered from his truck.

Ashleigh gathered her papers and ran to join Mike. It was an hour drive to Churchill Downs, and they filled the time with talk of Renegade. Mike wanted to give the colt a week off to recover, then see how he was training before he entered him in any more races.

Ashleigh hoped that Renegade's poor race was due to an off day and that he would bounce right back to his former self. It was the end of March. There was still the Arkansas Derby, the Wood Memorial, and the Blue Grass Stakes coming up in the middle of April. Those major prep races would set the stage for who would be the favorites for the Kentucky Derby.

"How soon will we race Renegade again?" she asked the trainer.

Mike shrugged. "That depends on what we find out from the drug test and the vet check." He pulled onto the back side of Churchill Downs and stopped at the guard shack to check in, then turned to Ashleigh. "I know you'd love to have him run in the Derby, Ash. And your parents want Renegade to have a good race record so he can retire to stud and bring in good money," Mike said.

The guard opened the gate, and Mike pulled into the parking lot in front of the receiving barns. "If Renegade runs poorly in these big races, we're going to hurt his reputation," Mike continued. "There's no sense racing the colt over his head."

Ashleigh opened the door and got out of the truck, admiring all the sleek Thoroughbreds that walked down the barn aisles and on the hot walkers. She crossed her arms and scowled. How could they have misjudged Renegade so drastically?

"I'm going to get this colt ready," Mike said, opening the trailer doors. "I'll meet you out at the track if you want to start watching the workouts."

Ashleigh nodded and headed for the entrance to the racetrack. She found a good spot on the rail and settled in. For a moment she was able to forget about her troubles as she looked out over the beautiful infield of Churchill Downs toward the stately white twin towers that were such an identifying part of the old track.

Ashleigh couldn't keep the grin off her face as she watched the graceful Thoroughbreds gallop around the track with their wiry jockeys aboard. Someday that was going to be her! She was going to win her first race at Churchill Downs! Her thoughts were interrupted by the harsh boom of a man's voice coming from down the rail.

"Great work, Johnny!" the man hollered. "Thanks for the betting tip on your horse. I made some good money on that guy yesterday. That horse of yours has really turned around. I hear your boss decided to bring him to Kentucky to train?"

Ashleigh turned and was shocked to see Mr. Rolland's groom standing several yards away. He glanced in her direction, and she took a step back, hiding behind the big man next to her. She didn't know why she didn't want the groom to see her. He just gave her the creeps.

Ashleigh watched the skinny groom pick up his horse. She wondered if Mr. Rolland was there, too. The last thing she wanted to do was talk to the creepy trainer about Renegade's poor performance yesterday. But Ashleigh's curiosity got the better of her. She stepped out into the road, looking for Johnny. Her jaw dropped, and her heart skipped a beat when she spotted him. The horse the groom was walking looked exactly like Renegade!

The horse turned its head, and Ashleigh could see the full blaze running down its face. Maybe it was Royal Rebel, the horse she had been following in the Virginia paper. But what was Mr. Rolland's groom doing with the horse?

Ashleigh sucked in her breath as it all began to make

sense. Rebel's listed owner, Dave Rolland, *must* be related to Renegade's Tom Rolland! She took several steps toward the disappearing horse and groom, then broke into a trot. She wanted to get a better glimpse of the horse that looked so much like Renegade.

She turned the corner of the barn where she had last seen Johnny. Several horses were being walked between barns, but she didn't see the large bay colt anywhere. She quickly walked past several barns, staring down the long aisles to look for the horse, but after a few minutes it was obvious she had lost them.

Rebel had raced just yesterday. They must have brought him to the track to stretch his sore muscles and limber him up after running his race.

She stopped to ask several trainers if they knew where Mr. Rolland's horses were stabled, but nobody knew. It dawned on Ashleigh that the trainer was probably just bringing the horse in for the day and he was stabled in the receiving barns right where she and Mike had parked, but when she got there, no one had seen the weaselly little man or his groom.

Ashleigh crammed her hands into her pockets and huffed. She would have liked to have seen Royal Rebel in person after reading so much about him. She turned and walked toward the race office to see if they had posted the results of the weekend's races.

Mike hollered to Ashleigh from one of the shed rows as she passed by. "The jockey is here—I'm taking this colt to the track now. I'll be back in fifteen minutes, and we'll go check the results of Renegade's test," he said.

Ashleigh waved and continued on to the race office. She scanned the lists, looking for Rebel's race under Virginia's track information. She found Royal Rebel at the bottom of the list. Ashleigh's brows drew together as she looked at the results. Maybe there had been a mistake? Why would Rebel's owners enter the horse in an allowance race when his last few outings as a cheap claimer had proven so unsuccessful? Horses usually went down in class when they lost races—not up. Not only had they moved Rebel up in class, but the horse had won the race by five lengths!

Ashleigh's head spun with all this new information as she left the race office and went to the cafeteria to get a soda. She almost choked on her beverage when she scanned the crowd and locked eyes with Mr. Rolland. He quickly looked away, but Ashleigh walked right up to him. She had to find out about the mystery horse.

"Hi, Mr. Rolland," Ashleigh said.

The trainer tried to look away, but Ashleigh stood by his table, forcing him to acknowledge her.

"Oh, hello, Ashleigh," Mr. Rolland said. "What brings you to the track today?" His eyes shifted around the room and glanced furtively out the window.

"I came with Mike to deliver a horse," Ashleigh replied. "But I was wondering about a horse I saw your groom with today." She watched Mr. Rolland closely, noting the narrowing of his eyes and his nervous cough.

"Well," Tom Rolland hesitated. "You must be mistaken. Johnny isn't here today." His eyes cut to the window once more.

"But I saw him," Ashleigh argued. "He was with a big bay horse that looked like—"

Mr. Rolland's hands fluttered in the air like crazed birds. "No, no. You are mistaken. Like I said, Johnny isn't here today." He stood and excused himself, then left the cafeteria.

Ashleigh watched the trainer's departing form. Why would Mr. Rolland lie about his groom? Something strange was going on. And Ashleigh was determined to find out what it was.

11

On the drive home Ashleigh fired questions at Mike about Royal Rebel and Mr. Rolland, but Mike didn't know much about either horse or trainer. *At least Renegade's test results came back clean,* Ashleigh thought. There were no drugs found in his system. Now they had to wait and see what the vet found out after he examined the stallion, then they could decide how to proceed with Renegade's training.

The vet was just finishing when they arrived back at Edgardale.

"How is he?" Mike asked as he and Ashleigh stepped into the barn.

Dr. Frankel smiled. "The colt seems to be all right—just a little tired. I've given him a vitamin injection. You can start him back to training by Friday." Dr. Frankel patted Renegade's neck and shrugged. "I have no idea why he ran so poorly yesterday. Maybe he had a bit of a bellyache." The vet packed up his things, promising to check back later in the week.

"Well, what are our plans now?" Mr. Griffen asked the trainer.

Mike rubbed his chin and stared at Renegade as the horse stood placidly in his stall. "I agree with Dr. Frankel. Renegade looks pretty worn out. Let's lay him off to rest until Friday, then we'll have Rhoda give him an easy gallop."

"What about the Derby prep races?" Ashleigh asked. "Are we still going to shoot for any of them?" She looked anxiously between her parents and Mike. "The vet said Renegade probably just had a bellyache. That means he could go back to running well again in his next race, right?"

Mike gave Ashleigh a grin. "It sounds to me like somebody has a touch of Derby fever," he teased, then grew serious. He paused for a moment and drew a deep breath. "I know everyone was starting to hope that we might have a Derby horse on our hands, but in light of how things have been going this past week, I think maybe we better pass by the Derby prep races that are coming up in two weeks and just settle for a nice allowance race."

Ashleigh's heart sank. Mike placed a hand on her

shoulder. "I know this is disappointing to you, but we've got to do what's best for Renegade. If he springs back and races well, we've still got time to get on the Derby trail."

Ashleigh nodded. She knew Mike was right, but it still didn't stop her from being disappointed.

When Friday finally rolled around, Ashleigh was ready for it. She had been waiting all week for Renegade's next workout. Mike only wanted to gallop the colt slowly for two laps of the track, but he still needed her to pony the stallion over to the Wortons' track.

Ashleigh was careful as she bent over to run her pony strap through the stallion's bit. She was now familiar with all of Renegade's new tricks. It had been a couple of days since he had been able to surprise her with a nip. He seemed to have calmed down a bit since his last race.

Ashleigh was surprised that Renegade was behaving so well. *Maybe he would get back to his old self again now that they weren't trying to breed any mares with him,* Ashleigh thought. Anything would be better than this last horrible week.

"Why the long face?" Rhoda asked when they stepped onto the training track.

Ashleigh shrugged and fiddled with Stardust's mane. She wasn't sure she wanted to say anything to Rhoda. She didn't want the jockey to think she was blaming her for Renegade's last race.

Rhoda smiled gently. "Is something bothering you, Ash?"

They turned the horses down the track to warm up. Ashleigh sighed. "It's just that things were going so well, and I was starting to hope that maybe Renegade would be good enough for the Derby. And now . . . he's doing terribly, and the Derby just seems like a dream."

Rhoda leaned over and patted Ashleigh on the shoulder. "I know what you mean. I feel the same way."

Ashleigh's head snapped up. "You do?"

Rhoda reached down to ruffle Renegade's mane and nodded. "After I rode him in that first race, I really felt like he had something. He felt like he could beat any horse out there. But now . . ." Rhoda hesitated. "I don't know. . . . He just feels different."

Ashleigh felt the tears welling behind her eyes. "It's all my fault. I should have never let him breed Stardust. If he hadn't, maybe he'd still be racing okay, and we could have waited to figure out his problem later."

"Don't be too hard on yourself, Ash," Rhoda said as they turned the horses toward the inside rail. "He's behaving pretty well today. Maybe Renegade was just feeling funny last week and he's coming back around now."

Ashleigh watched Rhoda and Renegade gallop off. Renegade pulled slightly at the bit and tossed his head as he picked up speed. Ashleigh smiled. Maybe Rhoda was right. People had off days. Maybe horses had them, too? The Derby was a month away. They still had time to get Renegade back into the swing of things.

Ashleigh spent the next couple of days helping around the barn. She had wanted to go to the races with Mike on Saturday, but her parents felt that she was already pestering the trainer too much. She eagerly awaited her folks' trip to the feed store on Wednesday, knowing that they would bring her back the racing results for the past weekend's races. She had kept a close eye on the *Daily Racing Form* and knew that Royal Rebel had run at Turfway Park on Sunday.

When she stepped from the bus after school on Wednesday, Ashleigh ran up the driveway to the house. As promised, the race results were on the kitchen counter. She dived into them, finding Rebel's information under the Turfway results. Ashleigh's eyes widened as she read the statistics. Rebel had moved up in class and had won again!

She tossed the papers back onto the counter. It

wasn't fair! Royal Rebel was a cheap claimer. How could he be doing so well when Renegade, who had a great pedigree, was struggling so much? She made a mental note to look up Rebel's parentage before she went to bed that night. Right now she had to get out to the barn. Rhoda was due to arrive anytime.

Renegade was scheduled to breeze a half mile to leg him up for his race on Saturday at Keeneland. Mike had found a nice one-mile allowance race that he thought Renegade could easily win.

When Rhoda arrived at four o'clock that afternoon, Renegade was back to his old routine, bucking and kicking around his paddock and nipping at anyone unfortunate to get too close to the stallion.

"He's going to be a real pistol today," Mr. Griffen said as he legged Rhoda up on the big bay. "I hope we don't have another one of his runaway sessions."

Rhoda fastened her chin strap. "Me too." She winked at Ashleigh and maneuvered Renegade into place beside Stardust.

Together they walked the horses over to the Wortons' training track. Mike was waiting for them when they arrived. "I want you to go around once, then work him an easy half mile," Mike instructed.

Renegade tossed his head and snorted as they stepped onto the track. Ashleigh held him tight, but by the time she let go of his head, her right arm felt like it was ready to fall off.

"I've got him, Ash," Rhoda said. She trotted the big horse up the track, then broke him into a smooth canter.

Ashleigh watched their progression around the track. The second time around, Rhoda crouched low over Renegade's withers as they approached the half-mile pole, and the big colt took off, racing for the finish line.

"Not bad," Mike called to them when they had finished the workout and were stepping off the track.

Mr. Griffen smiled broadly. "He ran the half in forty-seven seconds. That's pretty decent for working on his own in this deep dirt." He shoved his hands in his pockets and beamed. "Maybe we're getting our old horse back!"

Rhoda leaned down to stroke Renegade's neck. She looked concerned. "Yeah, he ran a pretty good half, but he gave up pretty easily on the run out to the five-eighths pole. Usually he's straining at the bit all the way to the pickup point. Maybe we haven't been galloping him far enough. He seems to be tiring so easily these days."

Mike frowned. "Are you worried enough to scratch him?"

Renegade kicked up his heels as he stepped off the

track, and Rhoda laughed. "I think that was a *no* vote from Renegade!"

On Saturday morning Ashleigh was up early to make sure Renegade had his oats at least an hour before they left for the track. She didn't want him racing poorly again because of another bellyache.

Mike arrived at eight o'clock to haul Renegade to Keeneland. Turfway Park was finished racing until the fall, and Churchill Downs was only open for training at the moment. Most of Kentucky's Thoroughbreds would be competing at Keeneland for the next few weeks.

Ashleigh wondered if any of Mr. Rolland's horses would be stabled at Keeneland. Would Royal Rebel be there? She knew Tom Rolland wasn't listed as Rebel's trainer, but she suspected he was connected to the horse in some way. Why else would she have seen his groom with the horse, and why would a man with the same last name as the creepy trainer be listed as own-ing the horse?

Ashleigh frowned as she crowded into the backseat of the car with her brother and sister. She had forgot-ten to look up Rebel's parentage. Keeneland had an extensive library on the front side of their racecourse. Maybe she could visit it while she was waiting for Renegade's race and do some research.

When they reached the track, Ashleigh helped her parents locate Mike at the receiving barns, then took Rory up to the horsemen's cafeteria to get something to eat.

On the way back they cut through the barns, admiring the beautiful horses and the way some of the trainers had decorated their shed rows with racing colors and fancy flowering plants.

Ashleigh was just making friends with a pretty gray mare when Rory tugged on her sleeve and pointed.

"Look, there's Mr. Rolland's groom!"

Johnny hadn't seen Ashleigh, so she ducked into an empty stall, pulling Rory along with her. "Shhh," she cautioned her little brother as she stepped stealthily from the stall and motioned for him to follow her as she tracked the groom through several of the barns. He stopped at a tack room in barn sixteen.

Ashleigh stayed around to watch for a few minutes, but nothing unusual was going on. She wasn't sure what she expected to happen, but her instincts told her that something wasn't right in Tom Rolland's barn.

"What are we doing, Ash?" Rory asked. "Are we playing hide-and-seek with Johnny?"

Ashleigh frowned. "Yeah, and he's no fun to play with. The game's over." She glanced at her watch. If she didn't get back to the receiving barns soon, her parents would wonder what she was doing. Since Ashleigh wasn't exactly sure herself about why she was sneaking around and spying on Mr. Rolland and his groom, she didn't want to have to explain anything to her parents.

She took Rory's hand and made their way back to Renegade's stall. Maybe there would be time after Renegade's race to walk down and pay a visit to Mr. Rolland? At least she knew where he had his stabling now.

Mr. Griffen waved to Ashleigh as he turned up the barn aisle. "Mike's got things covered back here. Let's go over to the front side. Renegade runs in the fifth race today."

Ashleigh nodded. She was anxious to get over to the track's library. She followed her family to the grandstands, excusing herself to go do her research.

"Can I go, too, Ash?" Rory begged. "You do all the fun stuff!"

"Where are you going, Ash?" Mrs. Griffen asked. "I don't want you wandering too far. You know where we'll be in the clubhouse."

Ashleigh nodded as she took Rory's hand. "We'll be in the library. I'll check back before Renegade's race."

She cut across the grandstand, pulling Rory in the direction of the library. When they stepped through the doors, she breathed deep of all the wonderful books. What a great idea it was to put a library at the racetrack. Especially when it held all kinds of wonderful research manuals on anything horse related!

Ashleigh went straight to the stallion directories, looking up produce records of sires for the previous years. She thumbed to the back indexes, looking up the name she wanted. Royal Rebel was listed there. Ashleigh felt her heart jump into her throat when she saw the sire listed for Rebel. It was Rabble Rouser—the same sire as Renegade! Her finger quickly traced across to the horse's dam. She felt a cold sweat break on her brow, and her stomach felt squishy. Royal Charm was the dam.

Ashleigh closed the book and took the nearest seat before her knees gave way. *Royal Rebel was a full brother to Renegade!*

Ashleigh looked at Rory, curled on a nearby chair, happily reading a book about a pony. It made sense that Mr. Rolland had never mentioned Rebel to the Griffens since he was racing so poorly—especially when he was trying to sell Renegade to them.

Ashleigh heaved a sigh. Maybe she was making something out of nothing, she thought. Most horses had siblings. Full brothers and sisters didn't necessarily have the same racing talent. She glanced at her watch. They had one more race to wait before Renegade's turn. "Come on, Rory," Ashleigh said. "Let's put your book away and go watch some of the races."

Ashleigh took Rory by the hand and led him from the library.

"Let's go watch the televisions," Rory said as he pointed to the far wall, where they showed the simulcasts from several other tracks.

Ashleigh looked over the multiple screens. They were showing races from the East and West Coast.

"Oh, oh!" Rory pointed to the end television set. "We're missing Renegade's race."

Ashleigh's heart jumped as she looked at her watch. "No, Rory, we've got another ten minutes before the horses even reach the saddling paddock."

"Nope." Rory shook his head vigorously. "He's right there on the racetrack."

Ashleigh looked at the screen and swallowed hard. The horse on the screen looked just like Renegade, but he was racing at a track in West Virginia. It had to be Royal Rebel!

The sound for the West Virginia track television was turned off so they could air a big stakes race in

California. Ashleigh couldn't hear any of the horses' names, but she was sure that horse had to be Rebel. She looked around to see if she could find her parents. She wanted them to see this horse, but she didn't want to leave to go find them. If she did, she would miss the race herself.

She watched as they loaded the horses into the gate. Royal Rebel broke well and followed the leader into the first turn. Ashleigh's heart jumped as she watched the horse's long-legged strides carry him out of the turn and down the backstretch, still hanging on to second place. The colt's style was a lot like the way Renegade had raced before his last failed attempt at running wire to wire.

"Go, Renegade!" Rory hollered. He tugged on Ashleigh's sleeve. "Why aren't we out there at the rail watching him?"

Ashleigh kept her eyes glued to the screen as Rebel took the lead heading into the top turn and stretched out his lead down the homestretch to beat the other horses by five lengths. "That's not Renegade," Ashleigh explained to her little brother. "That's another horse that looks exactly like him."

Ashleigh studied the screen as they showed the horses pulling up from the race. She was amazed at how much he looked like Renegade. His white blaze didn't seem quite as wide, but it could have been the angle of the camera. She still wondered how a cheap claimer could go from losing cheap races to winning stakes races easily.

"Who's that big guy holding that horse in the winner's circle?" Rory said, pointing to the television.

Ashleigh felt her stomach tighten uncomfortably as she recognized the large man who had blown the tire down the road from Edgardale over a month ago. No wonder the horse he had in the trailer had looked so much like Renegade. He must have been hauling Rebel to the racetrack when he got the flat tire near their house.

With one last look at the television screen, she grabbed Rory and pulled him in the direction of the saddling paddock. "Come on, Rory. Renegade's on his way."

Why did all the information about Royal Rebel bother her so much? Ashleigh wondered. Was it because Rebel was doing so much better than Renegade now? Or was it just because Mr. Rolland was involved and she didn't trust the weasely man? She felt like she should know the answer. It aggravated her that she didn't.

They arrived at the walking ring just as Renegade was being led around. The big colt looked great. Ashleigh was hopeful as she watched Renegade prance around the walking ring. Even Mike was smiling when he joined her and Rory at the rail for the post parade.

"He's not sweated up as bad as he was two weeks ago," Mike commented. "I think everything is going to work out this time. I gave Rhoda the same instructions as last time. She really needs to keep a tight rein on Renegade right from the start. I don't want a repeat of his last race."

But when the gates popped open for the one-mile allowance race, Renegade broke on top, fighting Rhoda for the bit.

"Get ahold of him, Rhoda!" Mike hollered as the horses thundered past them, racing for the first turn. Mike looked at the tote board. "They ran the first quarter in twenty-three flat. That's not exceptionally fast, but Renegade's still in the lead by three lengths." He pounded his fist on the railing. "I can't figure why this horse has changed his racing habits."

Renegade got the first call all the way to the three-quarter-mile pole, then once again he dropped back as if he had a five-hundred-pound weight tied to his tail, finishing many lengths behind the last horse.

Ashleigh's heart was breaking as she watched Renegade stand for her father while Rhoda removed her tack. The broken look on her father's face made her heart sink. This race had been so important, and

Renegade had blown it.

She wiped at the tears that were gathering in her eyes. What would become of Renegade now? Even though he had been perfectly rotten the last couple of weeks, she still cared about what happened to him. If her parents sold him, she hoped he didn't get another owner like Mr. Rolland. He deserved better than that.

The car ride home was uncomfortable. Everyone sat in stunned silence, trying to figure where they had gone wrong. Caroline and Rory fell asleep. Ashleigh lowered her head, hoping to catch a quick nap and forget about Renegade's failure for a while, but she was too anxious to sleep. After a few moments she heard her parents talking in low voices in the front seat.

"What are we going to do now?" Mrs. Griffen asked as she placed a comforting hand on her husband's arm.

Mr. Griffen shook his head wearily. "I don't know, but it's obvious we can't keep running Renegade in these stakes and allowance races. He's getting beaten badly. Every time he loses, it looks worse and worse on his record." He sighed heavily. "Nobody wants to breed to a stallion with a bad race record."

Mr. Griffen remained silent for several moments until his wife prodded him to speak.

"What do you think is the matter, Derek?" Mrs.

Griffen asked in concern.

Derek Griffen ran a hand through his dark hair, tousling it into disarray. "I think our best bet is to get rid of Renegade now and cut the losses for Edgardale."

Ashleigh wanted to speak up, but then her parents would know that she had been eavesdropping.

Mrs. Griffen placed her fingers over her husband's hand as it rested on the steering wheel. "Are you sure, Derek?"

Mr. Griffen nodded. "We've already got several mares bred to Renegade. Those foals will be worth nothing at the sale. We've spent money entering races that we got nothing out of. Edgardale has already been affected enough."

Ashleigh sat in the backseat with her eyes closed and her heart pounding in her ears. A single tear slipped down her cheek. How could they all have been so wrong about Renegade? She choked back a sob. Everything was falling apart, and there was nothing she could do to stop it.

12

Spring break was really off to a lousy start, Ashleigh thought the next day as she sat under the big oak tree with her pile of *Daily Racing Forms* and horse magazines. Only a short time ago she had hopes of racing Renegade in the Kentucky Derby. Now she would probably watch it on TV while Renegade stood in the barn, munching hay.

Several of the yearlings cantered up to the fence to see what Ashleigh was doing. They nipped and kicked each other, and Ashleigh laughed at their antics.

Slewette's new filly nickered to the yearlings, but she wasn't brave enough to face them all. She stepped behind her dam and peeked out from around her tail. Ashleigh was amazed by how much the tiny filly looked like Georgina's yearling. In another year and a half they would be about the same size and it would be difficult to tell them apart.

Ashleigh's mind began to wander. Would it be possible to switch look-alike horses in a race? She had heard stories from the grooms and trainers at the track about that sort of thing. Running in a ringer was what they had called it. It was usually done to make money betting on a horse. The less talented racer would race several times until his odds were very high, then his talented look-alike would be thrown in the race, the schemers would place their bets, and when that horse won, they would get rich.

Ashleigh frowned. All those stories had come from the old days, before all the new racing rules and blood tests.

The scene from the broken-down horse trailer flashed through her mind. She had been so sure that horse was Renegade and that he had been stolen. Her mind kept wandering back to Mr. Rolland and his groom. If anybody else had been connected with Rebel, it wouldn't have bothered her, but the fact that Mr. Rolland had owned Renegade and some relatives of his owned Rebel . . . Maybe it was more than coincidence.

"Hey, kiddo," Mr. Griffen said, coming up behind her. "Are you ready to help your mother and me move horses?"

Ashleigh nodded and stood up. "Mom, Dad,

would it be possible to switch horses for a race?" she asked.

Mr. Griffen's brows furrowed as he looked across the stable yard at his younger daughter. "Ashleigh, I know where you're going with this question," he said in dismay. "Don't try and make excuses for Renegade. Especially far-fetched ones." He looked at his wife and the rest of the family, who were just arriving for chores. "I guess now would be a good time to tell everyone. . . . Renegade just isn't the horse we thought he was. He's not working out for Edgardale, so we've decided to sell him. There's a buyer coming to look at the colt soon."

Ashleigh swallowed hard. She knew that's what her parents had been planning to do, but now it was official. She looked around at her brother and sister. Caroline didn't seem upset, but Rory looked like he wanted to cry.

Ashleigh's stomach flopped. Her mind was a jumble of mixed-up thoughts. She had the answer to Renegade's problem, and it was starting to form in her mind, but it seemed so far-fetched. She cleared her throat and asked her father insistently, "But if somebody *did* have two horses that looked alike. *Could* they be switched to race?"

Mrs. Griffen smiled patiently at Ashleigh and

shook her head. "Maybe back in the old days, but not with today's policies, Ash. Horses have to be blood typed, and the inside of their lips are tattooed. The paddock judge checks every horse's markings and tattoos in the saddling ring before the race. It would be almost impossible to run in a ringer," she said.

"*Almost* impossible," Ashleigh repeated. "But it *could* be done?"

Mrs. Griffen pursed her lips and gave Ashleigh an impatient look. "Ash, I know it's hard on you when we sell horses, but it's our only option for Renegade. We'll find him a good home. Now, could you get the stalls ready for Go Gen and Prize?"

Ashleigh headed for the barn, but instead of getting right to the stalls, she made a quick run to the barn's office to find Renegade's papers. She quickly jotted down his registration number on her hand, then grabbed a stool and went to Renegade's stall. "All right, you big bully," she said as she took the stud chain lead rope off the wall. "I need you to be nice for two minutes."

Renegade watched curiously as Ashleigh grabbed the stool used for braiding and pulling manes and set it in front of his stall. Ashleigh ducked quickly when the stallion reached out to snag her jacket. "Oh, no, you don't, buster. I'm on to your tricks."

Fortunately, Jonas hadn't removed the stud's halter yet, so Ashleigh quickly grabbed the stallion and ran the stud chain over his nose. She laughed when Renegade twisted his lips in a contortion, trying to nip her arm. She jingled the chain in warning, and the big bay settled down.

Ashleigh grabbed Renegade's upper lip and rolled it up like she had seen the paddock judges do. "Yuck!" she said as pieces of hay and saliva ran over her fingers. She looked at the black numbers that lined the horse's soft underlip. Several of them were difficult to read because part of the lining of Renegade's mouth was black like the numbers.

She could make out all the numbers correctly except for the last one. Renegade's registration papers said it was an eight, but Ashleigh thought it could be either a three or an eight.

Renegade shook his head, almost knocking Ashleigh from the stool. She lowered his lip and removed the stud chain. This time she wasn't quick enough, and the big bay snagged her jacket in his teeth. Ashleigh yelped and jumped away, brushing the slobber from the arm of her jacket. She glared at Renegade. "Okay, maybe I deserved that one, but it still wasn't very nice."

She frowned. Renegade had never bitten anyone

when he first moved to Edgardale. His manners were perfect. An idea came to Ashleigh.

"What are you doing, Ash?" Caroline asked when she walked into the barn and saw her sister holding the stud chain and the stool.

Ashleigh paused, trying to decide if she should tell Caroline her suspicions.

Caroline crossed her arms. "All right, Ashleigh Griffen. You're hiding something. Come on—spit it out."

Ashleigh hung the stud chain back on the wall. "Caro, I know it sounds silly, but I really do think that Renegade was switched. Everything started going wrong after I saw that broken-down horse trailer."

Caroline's brows rose. "What broken-down trailer?"

Ashleigh motioned for Caroline to follow her to the stalls she was supposed to be preparing. "I never told anyone but Jonas because I felt silly," Ashleigh admitted. She told her sister about seeing the horse trailer with the flat tire and the horse that looked like Renegade. "Mona and I came racing into the barn, screaming that Renegade had been stolen, but Renegade was in his paddock, and Jonas told me not to play stupid games like that. I felt really stupid," Ashleigh admitted. "But now I think that maybe the horses *were* switched."

Caroline rolled her eyes. "Come on, Ash. Mom and Dad already told you that it's impossible to switch horses in a race."

Ashleigh sighed. "I know it sounds crazy, Caro. But what if I'm right?"

Caroline handed Ashleigh a hay net. "And what if you aren't? If you think you felt stupid about telling Jonas Renegade was stolen, how do you think you're going to feel trying to convince the entire racing commission?"

Ashleigh crossed her arms, her lips a thin line of determination. The only way to convince anyone of anything was to get proof.

Ashleigh set her plans in motion the next day. Since her birthday was coming up, she got to pick how she wanted to spend it. Her entire family knew what that would be—a day at the races.

Ashleigh smiled as she spoke to Mona on the phone. "Mike's got a horse running that day, too," Ashleigh said. "So we'll have a good excuse to be on the back side. We'll find a way to sneak into Mr. Rolland's shed row and have a look around. If I could just get close to Rebel . . ."

"I hope we don't get caught," Mona said with a shiver. "That guy who fixed that flat tire looked awfully mean. I wouldn't want to see him again."

"Mr. Rolland is pretty creepy, too," Ashleigh said. "We'll just have to be very careful."

The next day when Mona and Ashleigh got back from riding the forest trails, Ashleigh's father was waiting for them.

"I need you to help me groom Renegade, Ash," Mr. Griffen said. "I've got a buyer coming to look at him in an hour." He smiled, trying to cover the bad news. "You're the best groomer I've got. I know you'll want Renegade to look good."

Ashleigh felt a lump form in her throat as she put away Stardust and got out the grooming kit for Renegade. They couldn't sell Renegade before she straightened out this mess, she thought. What if she was right? They needed both horses to prove which was which.

Jonas had Renegade hooked tightly into the crossties so that he couldn't nip. Ashleigh pulled up the footstool and started on the colt's shiny black mane. She fumbled the little comb, and it fell to the ground.

Mr. Griffen picked it up and handed it back to her. "I know this is hard on you, Ash, but we've got to do what's best for Edgardale. Renegade can't run, and we won't be able to get much of a breeding fee out of him if he doesn't have a good race record."

Ashleigh nodded. She continued down Renegade's mane, combing out the tangles. When she got three-quarters of the way down his neck, Ashleigh started picking through the colt's hair. Where was the little white patch of hair? Caroline had pulled Renegade's mane before his last race. Had she pulled out all of the white hairs? Renegade's mane was all black!

Ashleigh continued to look through Renegade's mane, but she couldn't find the small patch of hairs. Her heart quickened as she remembered the scar on Renegade's front pastern. She got off the stool and dropped to her knees beside the stallion. Renegade snorted and swung his head to nip, but the crossties pulled him up short.

"Careful, Ash," Mr. Griffen warned. "What are you doing?"

Ashleigh felt the back of Renegade's right front pastern, searching for the small, thin scar she had found when he first came to Edgardale. "Renegade has a scar," she said as her fingers frantically moved over the horse's ankle. Ashleigh sat back on her heels. "It's not there," she said, truly amazed that she couldn't find it.

Mr. Griffen came around to Ashleigh's side and knelt on the ground next to her. "Where are you looking, Ash?"

"Right here." Ashleigh pointed to the back of the pastern. "When Renegade first came to Edgardale, I was brushing him and I found some white hairs in his mane and a scar on his pastern. They're not there now." She looked at her father in alarm. "This horse isn't Renegade."

"I know there was a mark there when we vet checked this horse, but it could have been a healing scab from a scratch, and now it's gone." Mr. Griffen took Ashleigh by the arms and stood with her, making her meet his eyes. "Ashleigh, I know how desperately you want Renegade to stay at Edgardale, but you've got to stop playing this game. No one switched the horses."

Ashleigh felt tears spring to her eyes. She knew what her father was saying could be true, but she felt in her heart that this horse wasn't the real Renegade. She had bonded with the stallion when she had first met him. Her heart told her this wasn't the same horse.

"But Dad," Ashleigh cried. "There was a broken-down horse trailer in front of our house. . . ." The words began to tumble out unchecked as Ashleigh choked on her sobs. "I . . . I saw the horse, and he looked just like Renegade, only when Mona and I ran home to tell you, Renegade was in his stall. But that's when he began to act funny, and he started losing races. You should see Royal Rebel. He looks just like Renegade!"

Mr. Griffen pulled Ashleigh into his embrace, smoothing her hair as he tried to comfort her. "Look, Ashleigh, we've had a rough go with this stallion. We did the research, and we thought we had a champion, but we were wrong. It's time to admit that."

He pulled a handkerchief from his pocket and handed it to Ashleigh. "With today's technology and all the precautions that are taken with registration, it's nearly impossible to switch horses. You've got to let go of this crazy idea."

Ashleigh quieted her sniffles. There was no sense arguing with her father until she had real proof. And she was going to get it.

13

Saturday couldn't come fast enough for Ashleigh. She was out of bed and reaching for her jeans as soon as she heard the Wortons' rooster crow. Her real birthday wasn't for a couple of days, but this was the day for her birthday wish. She ran downstairs and joined her parents for a breakfast of toaster waffles and canned peaches—one of her favorites. As she ate, Ashleigh flipped through the Keeneland racing program. She almost dropped the orange juice carton on the floor when she read the entries for that day. Royal Rebel was slated to run at Keeneland in the sixth race!

There was no way they could hide the horse now, Ashleigh thought. But it would definitely make it more difficult to get in to see him. The Thoroughbreds were always well guarded the day of their race.

Her mind was a jumble of ideas as she worried

about how she was going to find Rebel once they got to the racetrack. Ashleigh's thoughts must have registered on her face because her mother spoke up.

"Ashleigh, I know you're really upset about Renegade, but you've got to stop with this idea that Renegade was switched," Mrs. Griffen said. "There's always somebody here at the farm. How could Renegade have been switched?"

Ashleigh felt the waffle stick in her throat. She swallowed hard. "But I saw the horse in a horse trailer," she said. "There was a horse trailer broken down outside Edgardale. Mona and I went to see if the man needed help. The trailer looked a lot like Mr. Rolland's, and the horse inside looked like Renegade."

Mr. Griffen put down his fork and ran a weary hand across his face. "Ashleigh, have you ever thought that maybe the horse in the trailer was Royal Rebel? You told us there was a horse that looked like Renegade. Who said there had to be a switch?" He leaned forward onto his elbows as he looked at Ashleigh's pained expression. "Maybe the man was hauling Rebel somewhere and they broke down in front of Edgardale."

Ashleigh took a deep breath, trying to hold back the flow of tears. Why wouldn't her parents believe her? "But you guys were both out in the back field that day, and Jonas was at the feed store for a while," she argued. "That's when the switch could have been made. That's when Renegade started acting funny and losing races."

"Ash . . ." Mrs. Griffen sighed.

Mr. Griffen tossed his hands in the air. "All right, I've heard enough of this. Ashleigh, let's just forget about this nonsense and try to have a nice day at the races. Okay?"

A tear slipped down Ashleigh's cheek, and she reached up to brush it away. Why didn't anyone believe her?

Ashleigh felt like she had a swarm of butterflies flying around inside her. Mike's horse had just finished second in the first race of the day, and her parents had let her and Mona go to the back side to see if the trainer needed any help. Once they were finished cooling out the horse, Ashleigh would have to find a way to get over to Mr. Rolland's barn and locate Rebel.

She held the hot horse while Mike bathed it. Then she and Mona led the horse over to the hot walker, and Ashleigh asked Mike if it was okay for them to walk around and look at all the horses.

"Sure," Mike said. "Just be careful, and be back here in another hour. I told your parents I'd get you back to the front side by the fifth race."

Ashleigh went to the guard shack to ask where Rebel's trainer's stalls were. It was surprising how easy it was to get the information. The guard looked on his clipboard, then pointed to the receiving barns, giving them the stall number. Ashleigh felt her stomach lurch. The hard part was going to be sneaking into the barn without anyone seeing them. "Come on," Ashleigh said to Mona as she led the way.

They cut through several shed rows, being careful not to attract too much attention.

"There it is." Mona pointed to a stall at the end of the receiving barns.

"And there's Mr. Rolland," Ashleigh said as she pulled Mona back around the corner. "I knew he was involved. Now I know something is going on!"

"What should we do?" Mona asked.

Ashleigh thought for a moment. "Let's wait and see if they leave. All I need is a minute. If I find the scar and the white hairs, I'll know it's him."

"Then what?" Mona shoved her hands deep into her pockets and peeked around the corner of the barn. She gasped. "There's the horse. He really does look just like Renegade!"

Ashleigh poked Mona on the shoulder. "That's because I think it *is* the real Renegade," she said in exasperation. "If I find the proof, we'll tell Mike. Maybe he can help me convince my parents. One thing's for sure—we've got to solve this case today. I think that buyer that came to look at Renegade the other day wants to buy him. Once Renegade and Rebel are both out of our hands, there's nothing we can do."

"They're coming this way!" Mona said in alarm.

Ashleigh cut around the corner of the building, hiding behind a pile of hay that was stacked near the shed row. Mr. Rolland and Johnny strolled by on their way to the cafeteria. Ashleigh gulped when she recognized the large man with them as the guy who had fixed his flat tire in front of Edgardale. They waited until the trio disappeared.

"Now's our chance," Ashleigh said as she crept out from behind the hay pile.

Mona hesitated. "Are you sure you want to do this, Ash? What if we get caught?"

"We've got to," she pleaded. "For Renegade's sake." Ashleigh turned and ran to Rebel's stall. She didn't care if Mona came or not, but she was glad to find her friend right behind her when she reached Rebel's stall.

The large bay stallion poked his head out the door when he heard the patter of feet in the shed row. He nickered and stuck his nose into Ashleigh's hair, whuffing softly.

Ashleigh's heart pounded in her chest. This was how the real Renegade always greeted her! "It's him!" Ashleigh said with a smile. "I know it's him!" She opened the door and stepped inside, letting Mona in with her. "Lock the door behind us so he doesn't get out," Ashleigh instructed.

Mona reached over the door, stretching to find the latch on the bottom half of the swing door. She found the bolt and shot it into place. "Better hurry, Ash. We don't know how long those guys will be gone."

Ashleigh stood on her toes and searched through the bay stallion's mane. Sure enough, she found a small patch of white hair. "They're here!" she cried in triumph. "The white hairs are here!"

She dropped quickly to her knees in the straw. The big colt nuzzled the back of Ashleigh's head. Ashleigh giggled. "If this was the horse that we have back at Edgardale right now, he'd bite my head off."

The girls laughed, then covered their mouths to stop the sound.

"There it is," Ashleigh said with a smile as her fingers traced the outline of a thin scar. She stood and threw her arms around the stallion's neck. "This is the real Renegade. I knew it!"

"Ash!" Mona said in alarm. "Someone's coming!"

They could hear heavy footsteps coming down the aisle. It was too late to leave the stall. Ashleigh pointed to the corner at the front of the enclosure. If they knelt in the corner, they couldn't be seen from outside—unless someone entered the stall.

Ashleigh squished down in the corner, making herself as small as possible. Her heart beat so loudly, she was sure it could be heard from several feet away. She looked across at Mona. Her friend looked terrified. The footsteps stopped in front of Renegade's stall, and Ashleigh thought Mona looked ready to faint. All the color had drained from her face.

"Time to close you up so you don't get too excited," a gruff male voice said.

A moment later everything went dark as the top door banged shut and the latch slid into place.

Ashleigh sat in the dark stall, listening to the ragged sound of her own breathing as she waited for her eyes to adjust to the dim light that filtered in through the cracks in the door.

"Are they gone?" Mona whispered.

Ashleigh sat still for another moment, listening for the sound of movement outside the door. All she could hear was the sound of retreating footsteps. "I think so."

"What are we going to do now?" Mona cried as she

crawled in the straw to sit next to Ashleigh.

Renegade nickered and stepped forward, blowing softly into the girls' hair as he nuzzled them.

Ashleigh reached up to stroke his soft nose. "Let me think a minute," she said. "We've got to find a way out of here. If we're in the stall when they come back to get Rebel—I mean Renegade—ready for his race, we're in big trouble!"

Ashleigh squinted and looked around the barn. "The walls are only about seven or eight feet high," she said. "It looks like there's a big gap at the top. If we could get over the wall, we could get out."

Mona huffed. "We're barely over four feet tall, Ash. How are we going to get over that wall?"

Ashleigh stood and brushed the straw from her jeans. "You could stand on my shoulders," she suggested.

"Good idea!" Mona waited for Ashleigh to bend down. She stepped onto her back, then shifted her balance as Ashleigh stood and moved to her shoulders. "I can reach the ledge," Mona said. But try as she might, she couldn't pull herself over the rim. Mona dropped to the ground. "You try it."

Ashleigh shook her head. "You're just as strong as I am. If you couldn't do it, neither could I." She glanced around the stall, looking at the buckets. "There's got to be a way to get higher. Maybe if I stood on one of the buckets?"

Mona shook her head. "It was shaky enough when you were standing on the ground, Ash. I don't want to break my arm if I fall."

"I've got it!" Ashleigh cried in a loud whisper. "Give me a leg up on Renegade and lead him over next to the wall. I'll be tall enough from his back to go over!"

Mona looked at the big colt and frowned. "I don't know, Ash. What if he bucks?"

"He'll be fine," Ashleigh said confidently, but the truth was, she was a little worried herself about standing on the stallion's back. "Come on. Let's do it."

Ashleigh stroked Renegade's neck, speaking calmly to him. "I think he'll be all right," she said. "Give me a leg up now." She grabbed a handful of mane and bounced several times before leaping onto Renegade's broad back.

Ashleigh sucked in her breath and clamped her legs tight against Renegade's sides as the stallion surged forward, making a quick round of the stall. "Whoa, easy," Ashleigh said, her heart jumping in her chest.

Renegade's ears flicked back to listen, and he slowed his step, stopping in the middle of the stall.

"See if you can lead him over to one of the walls," Ashleigh said. "Get him as close as you can." She waited while Mona grabbed Renegade by the nose and cheekbones and led him to the back wall. When the big colt held steady, Ashleigh shifted her weight and got to her feet, reaching for the top of the hind wall. "I've got it," she grunted as she pulled herself over the top.

Renegade snorted and jumped to the front of the stall.

"Hurry, Ashleigh," Mona cried. "I'm really scared. We've got to get out of here before those men come back."

The stall on the other side was empty. Ashleigh dropped down to the dirt floor, wincing at the pain in her knees. She quickly unlocked the door, glancing down the shed row to make sure no one had seen her. She peeked around the corner of Renegade's aisle and unlocked the stall to let Mona out.

"Come on. Let's get out of here!" Mona cried.

Ashleigh cut down a shed row. "We've got to tell Mike. He'll know what to do. Then we've got to find my parents and convince them that Rebel here is really our Renegade." Ashleigh glanced at her watch. Mike had expected them back at his barn five minutes ago. She moved as fast as she could go down the shed rows without spooking the horses. When they entered

Mike's stall area, he was pacing back and forth, looking at his watch.

"You're late," Mike said as he looked from Ashleigh to Mona.

Both girls started gabbing at once.

"Hold on there." Mike raised his hands for silence. "What's going on?"

"You tell him, Ashleigh," Mona encouraged.

Ashleigh started with the horse trailer incident and finished with finding the scar and white hairs on the horse in the receiving barn.

Mike scratched his head and rubbed his chin. "That's a mighty wild story, Ashleigh. Are you sure of your facts? This is a very serious accusation you're making. Some people are going to get hurt if it's true."

The ten-minute call to the gate for the sixth race sounded over the speaker system. Ashleigh took a deep breath and squared her shoulders. "I'm sure, Mike. I'd stake Edgardale on it."

Mike smiled and ruffled her hair. "Well, if that's the way you feel about it," he said seriously.

Ashleigh breathed a sigh of relief. At last someone who believed her.

Mike pointed to a young groom with straight blond hair. "That's Annsley. She'll make sure you get over to your parents okay. I'll go talk to the track security guards before the race starts." He smiled encouragingly. "Don't worry, Ash. We'll get this sorted out."

Ashleigh and Mona followed the young groom over to the front side. They were careful to walk to the rear of the horses filing across for the sixth race. They didn't want Mr. Rolland or Johnny to see them.

Mr. and Mrs. Griffen knew something was wrong as soon as they set eyes on the two girls. "What happened?" Mrs. Griffen asked in alarm. "You two look like you've seen a ghost."

Rory tugged on her sleeve. "How come you're all dirty, Ash?"

Ashleigh brushed at the dirt on her jeans from where she had crawled over the wall. She cringed when she thought of the danger she had just put herself and her best friend in.

"Mom, Dad, I need you to hear me out before you say anything." Ashleigh looked from one parent to the other, then took a deep breath and began. "I know you are having a hard time believing that Renegade might have been switched, but I've got proof now."

"Ashleigh," Derek Griffen interrupted, but quieted when his wife placed a staying hand on his arm.

Ashleigh continued. "Royal Rebel is entered in the sixth race, only it's not really him—it's Renegade. I got into his stall, and he recognized me. He's got the white hairs and the scar!" Ashleigh cried. Now she could see she had her parents' attention.

"You went into another trainer's stall?" Mrs. Griffen looked aghast.

Ashleigh hung her head. "I know I shouldn't have done it," she admitted. "It was really a stupid thing to do, but I had to do it for Renegade! Mike's on the back side, talking to security right now."

Mrs. Griffen looked at Mona to verify the events as Ashleigh was describing them. When Ashleigh was finished, her parents sat for several moments without speaking.

Mr. Griffen pulled his hat from his head and crunched it in his grip. "Ashleigh, what if you're wrong? A lot of people could get hurt here. We could even lose our racetrack license over something like this."

At that moment the trumpet sounded, calling the horses to the post. The horse that was supposed to be Royal Rebel stepped regally onto the track, his head held high as he pranced beside his pony horse.

"It's him," Ashleigh said.

"Look." Rory pointed out the window. "It's Renegade. How come he's running again today? I thought he wasn't going to race anymore."

Even Caroline couldn't take her eyes off the bay colt outside. "Wow," she whispered. "They must be twins."

"His record says the horse we have back at Edgardale is Renegade's full brother but a year older," Ashleigh said.

Mr. Griffen frowned. "They may be full brothers, but it's uncanny for them to look so alike."

They all took their seats. This was one race that Ashleigh willingly watched from the grandstand with her family. She sat on the edge of her seat when the horses were loaded into the starting gate and held her breath when the gate popped and Renegade broke well, going to the front with two other horses.

The Griffens all yelled for Renegade, when Royal Rebel was the horse the announcer was calling. But Ashleigh didn't care if people thought her family was nuts. Their horse was running well.

The big bay held his position as the horses came out of the turn and down the backstretch.

"Look at him go!" Mrs. Griffen yelled over the din of the race fans. "That's the kind of race Renegade usually likes to run!"

The announcer's voice broke over the crowd. "Royal Rebel takes the lead as they come out of the last turn and down the homestretch. Raging Storm moves into second, challenging for the lead, but Royal Rebel pours it on and opens the lead by three lengths. It's Royal Rebel all the way!"

"Yes!" Ashleigh cried as the horse she was sure was Renegade thundered across the finish line several lengths in front of the second-place horse.

When the excitement died down, Mr. Griffen plopped his hat back on his head, a grave look on his face as they steeled themselves for the trip to the back side.

Mr. Rolland spotted them as they were passing by the guard at the track entrance. He did a double take, then cleared his throat. "G-Good afternoon, Mr. . . . Mrs. Griffen. Wh-What brings you out here on this fine day?" he sputtered.

Mr. Griffen didn't answer. He just tipped his hat and kept walking.

Ashleigh's stomach felt like it was doing somersaults.

"There's Mike." Mr. Griffen pointed to where the husky trainer stood with a large racetrack guard.

Mike waved them over to where he stood. "Gus here is going to handle Mr. Rolland and the other trainer. You'll need to come with me to the track stewards and racing commission."

They waited a few minutes for Mr. Rolland to step off the track with his horse. Gus stopped the trainer and pulled him to the side.

"What's this all about?" Mr. Rolland protested.

The large man beside him, who Ashleigh decided was Mr. Rolland's brother, tried to slip away, but the guard grabbed his elbow and commanded him to stay put.

Ashleigh could see the fear in the weaselly trainer's eyes when he spotted her.

"Just bring your horse and follow me to the test barn, Mr. Rolland," the guard said. "We've got a vet waiting to take a blood sample."

"I demand to know what is happening!" Mr. Rolland screamed. "This is an outrage!"

Another security guard joined the first one. He gave Mr. Rolland and his partner a warning look. "A complaint has been registered with the track officials," he explained. "We'll need to impound your horse and run some tests." He turned to the Griffens. "We'll need your horse also. Can you haul him to us this afternoon?"

Mr. Griffen nodded. "We'll go get him right now."

Ashleigh watched the security guard escort the two Rollands into the test barn with Renegade. "What now?" she asked Mike.

Mike led the way to the race office. "They're going to do DNA testing on both the horses to see how they're related. Renegade and Rebel will be impounded while they sort this thing out." Mike smiled at Ashleigh.

"Don't worry, kid. From everything you've told me and the race records I've seen, I think you've got a pretty good case."

"They're here!" Caroline hollered as Mike's truck rolled down the long driveway in a cloud of dust.

Mr. and Mrs. Griffen and Jonas came running from the barn, and Ashleigh sprinted in from the pasture where she had been fussing over Stardust.

Mike stepped from the truck with a big smile on his face and handed the envelope to Mr. Griffen. Ashleigh held her breath as she watched her father rip it open and pull out the official papers inside.

Ashleigh thought she would go crazy as she waited for her father to finish reading the pages.

"Well, I'll be . . . ," he said in awe as he finished reading the letter.

"Well?" Ashleigh could contain her curiosity no longer. "What does it say?"

Mr. Griffen smiled. "It looks like you were right, Ash, but the two stallions weren't just brothers—they were twins!"

"Twins?" Ashleigh was shocked. "I didn't know there were many twins that survived."

Jonas stepped into the conversation. "I've seen a few twins in my lifetime," he said as he rubbed his stubbly chin. "They're a real rarity, but some of them do survive. There was a twin racing out west a few years ago that actually won a few big stakes."

Mr. Griffen reviewed the letter he held in his hand. "It says here that the horses' lip tattoos were indiscernible. Their registration numbers were only one number apart, and that number was smeared."

Ashleigh remembered that the black underside of the impostor horse's lip had been dark and difficult to read.

Mike shoved his hands in his pockets and rocked back on his heels. "That was what enabled the Rollands to switch the horses," he explained "The racing commission has a signed confession from both the men. It seems they had a little help from a veterinarian friend who altered the horses' tattoos. When the foals were born, they knew one of them was stronger than the other. They hid the foals on their farm and waited to register them until they were both almost two."

Ashleigh knew that The Jockey Club wouldn't register any Thoroughbred later than its two-year-old year.

Mike continued. "At that time one of the foals was smaller than the other, so it was easy to believe that they could be a year apart. Since they were both registered to the same sire and dam, the blood work all checked out okay with The Jockey Club. The colts were registered as full brothers a year apart in age."

"But why didn't Mr. Rolland just race both horses himself?" Mrs. Griffen asked. "Why sell us Renegade and then switch horses?"

Mr. Griffen pulled his checkbook out of his pocket and tapped it. "We paid a lot of money for that stallion," he said. "Once Mr. Rolland had our money, he switched horses so he'd still have the horse that could win races. I bet he and all his friends won a lot of bets, too."

Ashleigh gasped. "The first time I saw Royal Rebel at the track, there was a man who told Johnny that he'd made a big bet on his horse!"

Mrs. Griffen looked shocked. "So he had *our* money, plus he got the share of the winner's purse, *and* he placed bets on the side and won big," she said in amazement.

Mike nodded. "And now somebody's come forward to say that they were planning to purchase Royal Rebel for a high price, so the Rollands would have gained a lot of money by selling the same horse twice and sticking you guys with the lesser stallion."

Ashleigh's head spun as she tried to sort it all out.

She wasn't sure if she ever would. She concentrated on the most important thing. "When do we get our horse back?" she said with a worried frown.

"Look," Caroline said as she pointed to the cloud of dust coming down the road.

As the vehicle came closer, they could see it was a horse trailer escorted by a police car. They waited while the vehicle pulled into the stable yard and one of Keeneland's race officials stepped out.

"I've got a special delivery here for the Griffen household," he said with a smile as he stepped to the back of the horse trailer and opened the doors.

Royal Renegade backed out of the trailer and stood with his head held high. He whinnied to the mares and arched his neck at their welcoming call.

"Renegade!" Ashleigh cried as she ran to his side and hugged his neck. She giggled as the big bay softly woofed her hair and nuzzled her cheek. "You're home to stay this time," she vowed.

Jonas took the colt's lead rope and returned him to his stall. The family gathered around Renegade's paddock to watch the big stallion show off to all the mares.

"So what are your plans now, Derek?" Mike asked, idly leaning against the fence.

Ashleigh couldn't contain herself. "Renegade's won his last two races for Mr. Rolland. He's still a great racer. We'll enter him in the Derby! And if he wins that, maybe we can shoot for the Triple Crown!" she said.

"Not so fast, Ash," Mr. Griffen warned, pulling the official paper from his pocket. "It says here the racing commission still has some investigating to do. It could take months. We can't race him until his papers are cleared."

No racing? Ashleigh felt her Derby dreams crumble into dust at her feet. The Derby would be over by the time Renegade was cleared. She hung her head and scuffed her boot at the ground. She startled when she felt a warm breath of air cross her cheek and Renegade poked her with his nose.

Mrs. Griffen came up behind her and wrapped her arm around Ashleigh's shoulders. "It's not so bad, Ash. We've got our horse back, and if I remember correctly, all those mares, including Stardust, were bred before the switch was made." She turned Ashleigh to face her. "Renegade has proved himself as a racer. It's time to put him to work doing what we bought him for in the first place—breeding beautiful new foals! The Derby will just have to wait until Renegade's foals grow up."

Ashleigh smiled thoughtfully. In all the fuss, she had forgotten that Stardust might be in foal. She kissed Renegade on the top of the nose and laughed when he curled his lip. Stardust nickered, and Renegade tossed his head and trotted to the corner of the paddock to visit with her.

Ashleigh could just imagine Stardust with Renegade's foal running by her side. Almost a purebred Thoroughbred! Her thoughts were interrupted as Renegade trumpeted and kicked up his heels, galloping around his paddock, his black mane and tail streaming behind him. Renegade would never get to run in the Derby, but to Ashleigh he would always be a champion.

CHRIS PLATT rode her first pony when she was two years old and hasn't been without a horse since. Chris spent five years at racetracks throughout Oregon working as an exercise rider, jockey, and assistant trainer. She currently lives in Reno, Nevada, with her husband, Brad, five horses, three cats, a llama, a potbellied pig, and a parrot. Between writing books, Chris rides endurance horses for a living and drives draft horses for fun in her spare time.